"APOLOGIZE TO THE LADY!"

"I ain't taking no orders from you, highpockets," Curly Bub Becasse snarled. "Tend to your own damn business!" He dropped a hairy paw to the Smith & Wesson .44 at his hip.

As Becasse was clearing leather, Ki reached out and yanked him off balance. The teamster gave a wild yelp, lurching, trying to bring his revolver to bear. Ki knocked it out of his hand and jammed the heel of his right hand into the man's face. Becasse dropped, momentarily stunned.

Even before the teamster hit, his helper was rushing Ki. Butcher knife in fist, Shukka dove swiftly, silently, blindsiding Ki and slashing mercilessly at his back. . . .

WESLEY ELLIS

LONE STAR

AND THE SUICIDE SPREAD

JOVE BOOKS, NEW YORK

LONE STAR AND THE SUICIDE SPREAD

A Jove book/published by arrangement with
the author

PRINTING HISTORY
Jove edition/November 1988

ISBN: 0-515-09808-6

Jove books are published by The Berkley Publishing Group,
200 Madison Avenue, New York, New York 10016.
The name "JOVE" and the "J" logo
are trademarks belonging to Jove Publications, Inc.

PRINTED IN THE UNITED STATES OF AMERICA

10 9 8 7 6 5 4 3 2 1

Chapter 1

The late fall storm, promised by an angry sunset, blew in shortly before dawn. A cold breath fanned down from the mountain peaks, bearing on its wings a mutter of distant thunder. The breath rose to a whisper, the whisper to a wail. The mutter deepened to an ominous rumble out of the north, then became an intermittent crackling roar approaching along the spine of the Cascade Range.

Heavy rains swept the northeast corner of California, drenching thicket and trail and upland plateau. Wooded slopes streamed water, turning the dark canyons below to black torrents, while barren summits were etched in stark relief by lightning-strikes. Through flood and flare threaded the ancient Lechuza Path—the Owl Path—so named because it was most often traversed by backtrail jaspers who preferred to do their riding by night.

1

The Lechuza was not a direct or easy route, but it had the advantage of winding across a remote, vast wilderness. Between the Warner Mountains of California and the timbered reaches of southern Oregon, the trail sought—and found—a hazardous terrain of dense chasms, desolate buttes, and 6000-foot elevations. The Modoc used it, and the Northern Paiute, and the rogues of many races from Spanish adventurers onward. But the Path was far older than they, its stones bloodstained since time immemorial, its chaparral faintly agleam in the stormy dark with the phosphorescent glow of moldering bones.

For a while the rain froze to sleet and icy hail, like a portent of winter to come, as thunder cannonaded louder and lightning sundered night into day. The twisting ribbon of the Lechuza Path showed like a furtive silver snake in a blinding flash which for an instant etched in bluish fire the forms of two riders.

One was Jessica Starbuck, astride a feisty and storm-jittered sorrel mare. Tall and lissome, in her twenties, Jessie was swathed in a mackinaw whose tan color nearly matched her long coppery-blond hair, which she had tucked up under the crown of her brown Stetson. Although the mackinaw covered her flannel shirt, denim jacket, and much of her jeans, it failed to conceal the firm thrust of her breasts or the sensual curves of her thighs and buttocks. And despite an expression on her face mirroring the exhausting effects of her long journey, the autumnal chill could not dampen the warmth of her sultry face with its high cheekbones, audacious green eyes, and the provocative if challenging quirk of her lips.

Close by rode her companion Ki, on a spirited Apaluche gelding as black as the soul of the storm.

He too wore a mackinaw. His hatbrim was tugged low, visoring features that appealed to women who liked their lovers tempered by experience. A lean-faced man in his early thirties, with bronze skin, blue-black hair and almond-shaped eyes, Ki had been born to the Japanese wife of an American sailor. When orphaned as a boy in Japan, he'd trained as a samurai and become adept in martial arts.

Upon immigrating to America, Ki had been hired by Jessie's father, Alex Starbuck, head of the world-wide Starbuck business empire. Consequently Ki and Jessie had virtually grown up together, and after her father's murder it seemed only fitting for him to stay on, but as loyal confidant to the young heiress. She took control of her huge inheritance and far-flung responsibilities, proving to be strong and capable, and harder than a keg of railroad spikes if need be. Working together, as close as any blood brother and sister, they made a formidable team.

Before long the downpour lost its frigid sting and waned to a drenching shower, which gradually slackened to a steady drizzle as the storm rolled on southward. Jessie and Ki relaxed, conversing in low tones and soothing their skittish, tuckered mounts. They'd ridden steadily for 300 miles from Reno, the nearest railhead, after an interminable trip by train and stage from Jessie's Circle Star Ranch in Texas. They'd had to buy the horses and gear, since Reno liveries insisted rental nags be returned in short order, but fortunately they'd found Jessie a tough, sure-footed sorrel, and Ki had picked a black that had sand and bottom to spare.

Half an hour later they reined up and dismounted for a stretch. Wind had pulled the murky clouds away from the moon; they could glimpse a distant sheen of river- or lake-water, and the flanking ridge-lines of mountains jagged against the sky. Ahead, the Lechuza Path wandered on north by northwest, while to its right, yonder across shadowed rises, winked a low-lying reddish star. Immediately their practiced eyes caught it as the glow from a lighted window.

Shivering, Jessie commented, "Wonder why anyone would get up this early."

"Or stay up this late," Ki noted, wringing out his hat. "Well, folks who rise early or bed late need to keep warm and dry, so I reckon we'd better head over and visit before whoever's up goes out or to sleep."

"Before I catch my death of cold, is more like it."

Remounting, they rode northerly as the first suspicions of dawn grayed the eastern horizon. The lighted window glowed a sickly yellow in the softening sky, but there was no other sign of life about the small ranch house set in a pocket of juniper trees. They pulled their horse to a walk, eyeing the single light meditatively, reluctant to awaken sleeping folk at such an hour, yet leery of riding up on lonely roosts unannounced.

After a moment's hesitation, Jessie shrugged and Ki called out a cheery "Hello the house!"

There was no answer. The house squatted silent as before, with its single open eye staring sullenly through the gloom. The lighted window was at the rear of the house, evidently opening from the kitchen, and they cautiously ambled around to the back. As they passed the window, they caught a distorted glimpse through the rain-streaked pane of men seated at a table.

4

"Eating breakfast, I suppose," Jessie said dubiously. "Odd, though: no smoke is coming out of the chimney."

"I didn't smell any, riding up, or any odor of cooking, either," Ki added as they pulled up at the back. "Maybe they go in for cold snacks."

Jessica dismounted, nodding. "Probably a night crew just in, scrounging a bite before sacking off," she suggested. Ground-reining her sorrel, she walked with Ki to the rear stoop and rapped loudly on the closed door.

The sound seemed to echo in the room beyond, but there was no scraping of pushed-back chairs. Again she knocked and waited, catching no response, glancing with puzzled concern at Ki. Frowning thoughtfully, Ki gripped the doorknob, turned, and pushed. The door swung back easily and they stepped into a lighted room. It was a kitchen, all right; but there was no fire burning in the cast-iron stove, nor was there any smell of food or steaming coffee.

At a large clawfoot dining table sat four men. Two sprawled in their chairs, heads lolling back, like men who lazily slept—but their eyes were open. The other two hunched forward, and the arm of one hung down by his side in a stiff, unnatural position.

Before Jessie could gasp out a word, Ki motioned for silence. For a long moment they stood quiet, straining to hear any sound inside the house while they scrutinized the strange foursome and the room around them. Deftly, then, Ki began to undo his mackinaw. Jessie too opened her wet mackinaw, and swung it back to free the butt of the custom Colt revolver holstered on her right thigh. She then

5

checked her two-shot derringer and, finding it dry, stashed it back in its cunning hideout behind the brass buckle of her belt.

Under his mackinaw Ki was range-clad in jeans, a loose, collarless shirt, and an old leather vest. He packed no firearm—he didn't care for them, as a rule—but he was anything but defenseless. Sheathed behind his waistband was a short, curved *tanto* knife; and for a belt he used a *surushin,* a six-foot cord with a leather-covered lead ball at each end; and stashed in his vest pocket were slim throwing daggers and *shuriken,* little razored steel disks shaped like stars.

Ki wondered, though, if he was equipped to combat this new threat. He'd seen the carnage caused by weapons such as his, had viewed many weird and grisly sights of their butchery; but he had gazed on none more macabre, nerve-rending, or ominous than the handiwork left in this room. For seated at that empty table near the cookstove were four men without visible wounds or other signs of violence, but with stiffened limbs and glazed, sightless eyes. They were starkly, chillingly dead.

Together, then, he and Jessie padded through the unlighted house. They found cleanliness and order, and signs of recent occupancy, but nobody else, alive or dead.

Going out through the rear door, they prowled around the yard and warily approached the bunkhouse, Jessie keeping her hand close to her pistol. The door opened readily to Ki's touch, and they peered at the made-up bunks and the cold stove. Closer examination showed a thin film of dust on the top blankets of the bunks, and there was a faint sprinkling of rust particles on the stove metal. The stable was likewise unoccupied, but stocked with hay and grain. There were stalls for a dozen horses, and these stalls interested Ki. Hoofmarks showed in the mud of a well-built corral, but due to the storm it was impossible to tell how long ago the horses had departed.

Fairly certain every living thing had departed, one way or another, Jessie and Ki went to where their mounts patiently waited, sheltered somewhat from the weather in the lee of the house. They led the horses into the stable, stripped them, and rubbed them down. But they did not hang their saddles and bridles on convenient pegs. Instead they put the gear back on, using an "owlhoot" rig with loose cinches and bits free, hanging ready to be slipped into place.

"Never can tell who might drop by," Ki remarked when they had done. "A wrist twist or two, now, and we can hightail out of here pronto."

"Like as not it'll come to that," Jessie responded, as their horses set to feeding. "Most anything is liable to happen where guys sit down to a drink and a bite and wake up dead."

They headed back to the kitchen. Carefully avoiding the table, they went and looked over the cookstove. There was no rust on its top, and when Jessie lifted a lid, she saw the frail pulsing glow of live embers scattered among the ashes in the firebox. She remarked, "This's been used since the stove in the bunkhouse."

Beside the stove was stacked some kindling and cordwood, which Ki used to relight the fire. As the kitchen began to warm up, they studied every inch of floor around and beneath the table, pausing every so often to glance out of one or another of the rain-streaked windows. Next they went over the bare tabletop meticulously, Jessie frowning as she bent low and peered at the smooth surface with narrowing eyes. Finally she stepped back, mulling restively and watching Ki rifle the bodies. Seeing the dead men seated stonily at their table gave Jessie the creeping queasies, but handling them apparently didn't bother Ki one whit, so she was determined to stick it out.

Using great care not to change their positions, Ki examined the corpses thoroughly, giving particular attention to their hands. After probing every pocket, noting the condition of guns and knives, and making sure none of them had suffered hidden wounds, Ki stood contemplatively for a moment, then sat down in a chair which had been placed near the stove.

"Well?" Jessie prompted.

"Well, five men sat down at that table, and one left it."

"I figured as much when we were checking the floor. Three men had on high-heeled boots, two pairs marked by spur clamps and stirrups, the third showing the runover heels and scuffs caused by walking more than riding. The fourth man wore square-heeled, laced boots. The fifth man, who isn't here anymore, was wearing house slippers or something like that."

Ki nodded. "I couldn't tag it closer, either, but the rest adds up. Two cowhands, judging from those ride-worn boots, and the rope and bridle calluses on their hands. One miner, from the looks of his calluses, the lace-up boots, and the rock dust in the linings of his pockets. And one having the telltale smooth hands, sanded fingertips, and pasty skin of a nighttime gambler."

"Sounds like they met by chance—or did they have anything in common?"

"A few nasty habits. They've no identification, no personals to trace them, but have oiled cut-out holsters, and the calluses on right thumb and forefinger that come from practicing the draw. Waddies, tinhorn, rock buster—and all four of 'em gunwolves. All a dead loss, now." Ki pursed his lips thoughtfully and glanced out the west window. Then suddenly he stood up, his gaze fixed on the window.

"But five up-and-coming gents are something else again!"

Chapter 2

Joining Ki, Jessie immediately spotted the cause of his alarm.

Through the window could be seen a ribbon of rain-washed trail, which joined with the slithering Lechuza a couple of miles distant. Along this trail, gigantic and distorted in the swirling mists, five men were briskly riding in the direction of the ranch house.

As the horsemen drew nearer, Jessie and Ki noted that one was an odd looking figure in a long black mackintosh and a hard hat. Congress gaiters were thrust into box stirrups, and he wallowed about in a high-cantled Pueblo saddle as if unaccustomed to horseback riding, although his mount was a superb Hambletonian trotter. His four companions wore musty yellow slickers and rumpled broad-brimmed hats with flat crowns—typical rainy-day workclothes, as common as the ordinary stock saddles and regular cow ponies under them.

There were heavy curtains to the ranch-house windows. Jessie drew them close while Ki shot the bolt on the other door. Then they waited. Soon they heard the soft chuck of horses' hoofs on the soft ground, then a popping of saddle leather and a jingling of bridle irons as the men dismounted. They clumped up the veranda steps, tried the locked door, knocked loudly, waited, and knocked a second time. There followed a rumble of unintelligible words, then a voice suggested:

"Let's try 'round back!"

They clumped down the steps. A moment later the kitchen door creaked open. Boots scuffed the floor. Then—

"Great fuckin' Jehoshaphat!"

There came a moment of tingling silence, then another man spoke, harshly, peremptorily: "Spread outta this, fast! Grampus, take the bunkhouse; Doyle, the stable with Hicks. Ingersoll, you and me'll go over this house. Shoot first and— Hicks, you idjit, open your slicker so's you can get at your iron! Now, y'all, shoot first and ask questions afterward!"

Feet moved, then froze as from the darkened inner room a voice spoke, low and even, and as menacing as the snarly cough of a cougar. "Suppose you stay put, gentlemen, and *answer* some questions first!"

They stared at the doorway, slack-jawed, foolishly. A statuesque young woman strode out, eyes glinting in the shadow of low-drawn hatbrim, right hand resting on the heel of her pistol as she stared back at them. With venom.

12

Three men, who had cowpoke written all over them, stood flummoxed and rattled in a muck of sweat, raising no threat to Jessie. The fourth, a lean gray-haired bantam looking tough, wiry, and hostile, minced no palaver but drew a .45 Remington as big as he was. His slicker billowed out some as he went pulling, giving Jessie a glimpse for a second of a tatty brown vest, to which was pinned a five-pointed star marked DEPUTY MARSHAL.

Ki too caught the flash of badge. It gave him pause, for he was disinclined to nail star-toters willy-nilly, yet he was cocked and ready, a dagger in hand, aimed at the deputy's belly. The deputy drew with the practiced skill of fifty years, unconsciously, completely economically, as though he were reaching for a piece of pie. But once his revolver was in his hand, he didn't seem to know what to do with it.

From the dark doorway behind Jessie, then, a sliver of steel winked out across the room. The fifth man loosed a terrified squawk. Standing with his mackintosh draped open and his hand thrust inside his suit jacket, he stared aghast at the protruding hilt of a dagger, which had sliced through his jacket pocket, skinning his ribs.

Even now, the gawking waddies didn't draw. Even now, the older gent facing Jessie with a puckery expression, thumb on the gunhammer, did nothing. It ran too gut-misery deep against their grain for these men, for most men, to break the code of their fathers and shoot a woman. Jessie knew that, of course. That was why she had come out and had Ki stay back; had they been met with shooting first, probably everyone would've been hash by now. For that matter, her venture here would've gone to hash, too; so it paid to be nice.

Ki emerged from the doorway, eyeing the hard-hatted dude for any more sneaky moves. He'd caught him once, grubbing for a hideout gun, and had winged the dagger he'd been keeping for the deputy. The deputy had balked like Jessie had predicted, but Ki had another dagger balanced in his left hand, in case the badge was bent or Jessie's theory was shot down—again.

"A little sidewinder de-fanging," Ki explained, mostly for the benefit of the deputy, who eyed Ki with a pained, puckered face, revolver held slackly, seemingly forgotten. Ki grinned at the hard-hatted gent, adding, "The next one will be closer."

The man eyed him askance. "Hardly much threat, coming from a skirtchaser who hides behind the skirts he's chased," he berated, removing his hand with a dismissive flourish. As he did so, he unwittingly snagged loose a stubby .32 Moore pocket pistol and swept it toppling out of his jacket to the floor.

"A-ha!" the lawman barked suddenly, and raked the hard-hatted man with a look of stinging disgust. "Pick up your popgun, Thaddeus, and stow it away. For good, mind. You pull hijinkery like that again, so help me Gawd I'll put it to you where the sun don't shine, and pull the trigger!"

Thaddeus stooped to grab his pistol, muttering darkly.

"He was obeying your order to shoot first," Jessie told the lawman, "and I'm not worrying about anything else. When it comes our turn to answer questions, I'm sure we'll do so satisfactorily. And if you

14

feel uncertain about us, we'll go with you and talk to your boss. Will that do, Deputy—?"

"Voight, Quentin Voight." The lawman glanced from Jessie to Ki to his revolver, which he then jammed in his holster. Sheepishly he said, "Guess I flapped my gums a mite hasty. Wal, here'n now that shoot first order is in the discards."

Introducing herself and Ki, Jessie asked, "And these others?"

Before Deputy Voight could answer, the man called Thaddeus horned in: "Thaddeus Ingersoll, president of Unity Valley Thrift and Loan. I've business with Yokum and no patience with your twaddle, whatever the reason. So just run along and fetch Yokum, or bring me to him, or—or can you? Egad, what've you done with Yokum?"

Jessie regarded Ingersoll frigidly. "Believe I mentioned you were going to *answer* a few questions, not ask them. Keep still unless spoken to."

Ingersoll blustered indignantly. The three cowhands snickered loudly, and even Voight twitched a smile as he introduced the trio to Jessie. "The big fat feller hiding behind the grin is Orville Hicks. That snake-on-stilts beside him is Jud Grampus. The li'l hungry-looking mug is Doyle, Latigo Doyle."

The waddies ducked their heads in acknowledgment. Then Jessie asked, "Know any of these four dead men?"

They shook their heads.

"How about this Yokum chap?" Jessie asked Voight.

Ingersoll started to speak, but the deputy silenced him with a peremptory gesture, and explained: "Yokum McQuade owns this spread. Mr. Ingersoll

15

holds a note on it, and a quarterly installment is due. We rode out to collect."

"You fooled me. I never saw a sheriff's posse ride 'round gathering loan payments before. Is it a local custom hereabouts, or does the bank hire you?"

The deputy snorted through his nose at her facetious remarks. "Ain't customary a'tall, but Yokum is a salty dog with a quick trigger. Him and Mr. Ingersoll had words on their last run-in, so when Mr. Ingersoll reported threats and asked for protection this morning, I figured a tagalong was in order to keep peace. These three dogie dodgers are sort of at loose ends right now, and they came along for the ride."

"Yep, nothin' much to do till we tie onto a job," Hicks said.

Doyle nodded agreement, then hesitantly asked, "Ma'am? Miz Starbuck, was you an' Ki ever been o'er Wyoming, around Euchre Buttes way?"

"Yes, briefly, a few years ago."

The others darted inquiring glances at Doyle, but the little cowhand did not choose to elaborate. They saw, however, that he looked at Jessie and then at Ki with something akin to marvel in his gaze. And Jessie quickly moved to another subject. Gesturing at the table, she asked, "I suppose you fellows know what time it began raining last night?"

Everyone nodded. Jessie went on, "Our horses and gear are in the stable. Go look at the rigs and you'll easily see that we were in that frozen downpour for quite a spell, from the start, in fact. And a look at the four bodies sitting right there will show you they've been dead for many hours and never out in the storm. Right?"

The deputy nodded, mulling.

"Which goes to show," Jessie continued, "that they got here before the rain started, and died before the rain started. That sort of counts me and Ki out of having anything to do with them, doesn't it?"

Without replying the deputy went and took hold of a dead arm. He scrutinized the rest of the body, then let the arm fall back stiffly. "I'm going out to the stable," he announced, and stalked out of the room.

A few minutes later he returned.

"You win," he told Jessie shortly, with grudging admiration. "There sure ain't much you and Ki missed. I'd wager most law officers couldn't do as well. But then," Voight added dryly, "most law officers don't hitch up hosses the way you got yours hitched. Sort of on the quick-getaway side, you might say. Mainly you might say where Yokum McQuade quick-gotaway to."

"He wasn't here when we arrived, just about daybreak," Ki responded. "Didn't McQuade have any cowhands? There's nobody in the bunkhouse. Beds haven't been slept in of late, either."

"Yokum let all his hands go a couple of weeks back," Voight said. "Didn't have but four—it's a good spread, but a small one. I understand he was short of ready cash and figured to make out during the slack season with his Mexican cook and a wrangler. Got mad and fired the cook and wrangler, too. Seems like he didn't hire anyone in their places yet. But where is he?"

"Why keep on fussin' about Ol' Man McQuade?" Jud Grampus asked. "He'll show up. Off looking for a hand or two, maybe."

"He'd better put in an appearance right promptly,"

Thaddeus Ingersoll declared stuffily. "If that payment isn't made in time, Yokum McQuade may lose more than a crew and cook."

Voight was about to reply when somewhere outside the house a faint shout sounded.

"Bet that's McQuade now," Hicks asserted.

They crossed to the living room window and Doyle drew the curtain aside. Rumbling along the trail, vaguely seen through the swirling rain mists, loomed a big freight wagon drawn by a six-mule team. Three figures occupied the wide seat. The body of the wagon was piled with trunks and bags.

Voight spoke over Jessie's shoulder. "That's Curly Bub Becasse, the teamster from Unity, and his helper Shukka, and—uh-oh, looks like a gal on the seat there with 'em!"

"Headed this way, too," Jessie said, turning to Voight. "You better warn her or stop her. Whatever this's all about, having her see it won't help."

Voight acted swiftly. "Shove the curtains back in here," he ordered. "Hicks, Doyle, go bolt the back door and draw those kitchen curtains. Shut the kitchen door. Sure can't let the li'l lady get a peek at the kitchen before we move to make those four gents there comfortable. Open the front door and do the talking, Ingersoll."

Up the trail rumbled the wagon, the big teamster whooping and cracking his blacksnake from time to time.

"Sounds like Curly Bub's got a snootful of rotgut aboard, as per usual," Grampus hooted.

Beside the veranda, Curly Bub Becasse pulled up. He flipped the multiple reins about the whipstock with an expert gesture, leaped solidly to the muddy ground and, reaching up, swung the girl from the seat onto the porch with effortless ease.

She hesitated, staring around with wide blue eyes, the water dribbling down her India-rubber raincape and squishing from her soaked button shoes. As Ingersoll flung open the door, she stepped forward, entered the living room, and stood glancing from one to another of the group. Her gaze focused on the eldest, Deputy Voight.

"Are you Uncle Yokum?" she asked in a hopeful warm voice.

"Reckon you mean Yokum McQuade," Voight responded heartily. "Afraid I ain't him, miss. Yokum is—is away on a li'l trip right now. You say he's your uncle?"

She nodded, flustered. "Yes. I've come here to live with him. Unk wrote he'd meet me at the stage depot, but he didn't show up or anything."

"Probably he just couldn't make it," Voight soothed. "But don't you fret, he'll be along in short order. Best thing you can do now is trot upstairs to whatever room you like and change into some dry clothes. C'mon, boys, let's get the lady's trunks off the wagon and carry 'em up to her."

They were moving toward the porch when the thick-set figure of Curly Bub Becasse loomed in the doorway, face stubbled and plug-ugly, muscle and beerfat bulging his grimy workclothes. Close behind padded his helper, Shukka, a long-shanked, bucolic-looking Indian wearing the tails of a greasy plaid shirt outside a pair of buckskin leggings, from which protruded the handle of a butcher knife.

Lumbering in, Becasse howdy'd everyone, favoring the women with a cheesy grin and a lift of his hat—and revealing a bare bald head. Shukka edged aside as he entered the room, watching with inscrutable eyes and deadpan features, cold, predatory—a red gash of a mouth, craggy high cheekbones, a vulture's curved beak for a nose. First his eyes fixed on Jessie, then on Ki alongside her, the tight lids drooping the merest fraction. Then Shukka shifted his stare to meet Thaddeus Ingersoll's eyes.

Ki, his gaze lingering on Shukka, sensed that there was meaning of some sort in the swift exchange of glances. The faces of both men remained expressionless, however. *Shukka* meant hog in Choctaw, Ki recalled, but this Shukka lacked the characteristic features of Muskhogean indians, of which the Choctaw are members. Somehow, though, the indian's general physique struck a familiar chord, and Ki consulted Jessie in a murmurous aside. She considered Shukka carefully and, sure enough, she conjured up the elusive memory.

"A well-nigh full-blood Katepwa," Jessie suggested, as the swarthy man sidled along the wall in a self-effacing manner. "Remember? Only a handful of the tribe survived, up in the Absaroka Mountains. Shukka is the spitting image of them."

"You're right. Makes me wonder how one of the last few Katepwa alive came to leave southern Montana and wind up here in the Far West," Ki muttered, but his attention was quickly turned to Shukka's boss, Curly Bub Becasse.

"Just a minute, here," the teamster protested. "The lady owes me for a li'l bill for freightin'."

"I told you, I have no money left," she explained, disconcerted. "I told you Uncle Yokum will take care of the charges as soon as he arrives."

"Uh-huh. But he ain't here."

"I'm sure he'll return shortly. If you'll just wait until—"

"Not a'tall; I don't mind a-waiting around—with *you!*" Becasse sniggered with an ogling leer.

The baiting got a rise out of the girl, Ki saw. He made ready to move. But Becasse failed to unnerve her, to bring her to blushing or bursting into tears. Instead, the girl drew herself up, stiffening, suddenly appearing older and maturer—and angrier. Her face hardened with indignation. Her right arm started to draw back, Ki saw, as though she had a blacksnake whip to crack. But she didn't get to haul off and paste Becasse one, because by then Ki had butted in.

Smiling amiably, Ki sauntered in front of her. "You don't need to wait for your uncle," he said, a steely note edging his mild tone. "Miss Starbuck and I were using his place today, so we owe him for shelter and horse feed. I'll just take charge of the bill for freighting your trunks, and he won't need to do any waiting around."

Curly Bub Becasse swelled like an enormous frog. "I ain't taking no orders from you, high-pockets," he snarled, frowning belligerently. "I'm waiting 'round as long as I please. Tend to your own damn business!" He dropped a hairy paw to the Smith & Wesson .44 at his hip as he spoke.

"Poor Curly Bub," Latigo Doyle sighed.

As Becasse was clearing leather, Ki reached out and yanked him off balance. The teamster gave a wild yelp, lurching, trying to bring his revolver up to bear. Ki knocked it out of his hand and jammed the heel of his right hand into a slobbery face. Becasse

21

lurched awry, his legs tangling, and dropped, momentarily stunned.

"Hey, that was a short, easy deal to work out," Ki remarked affably, standing over Becasse. "You're going to be paid by me, and you're going to apologize to the lady. Agreed?"

Becasse, face purpling with rage, launched himself off the floor, swinging a roundhouse right. Ki backed hastily, ducking Becasse's first and last punch, catching the teamster's outflung arm and angling to drop one knee, swinging him into a *seoi-otoshi,* the kneeling shoulder-throw. Becasse arched through the air, past the startled onlookers. There was a wild crashing of splintered wood and clang-jangling of shattered glass, then the sodden thud of the heavyset Becasse striking the wet earth a dozen feet below.

Even before the teamster hit, his helper was rushing Ki. Butcher knife in fist, Shukka dove swiftly, silently, blind-siding Ki and slashing mercilessly at his back.

Ki had already glimpsed Shukka drawing his knife, however. It was one of the reasons he had thrown Becasse; now he was able to pivot and lash upward with a high kick. Shukka caught Ki's heel smack on the chin, its impact so hard that it jarred the knife from his grasp. Ki, stepping forward with the momentum of his kick, grabbed Shukka's right arm and left shoulder, pushing while hooking his foot in slightly behind one leg. Toppling backward from the kick and sideways from the shove, Shukka fell into a *hizo-otoshi,* or elbow-drop, as Ki dipped to his right knee and yanked hard. The stunned Indian catapulted upside-down through the air and collapsed resoundingly on the floor, staring sightlessly up at the ceiling.

Voight, Ingersoll, the girl, and the waddies gaped dumbfounded at Shukka, at the demolished window, at Ki. Jessie took the knife and pitched it out the front door. Brushing himself off, Ki turned to the girl with a rueful grin and a hint of the merry devil in his eyes.

"Sorry, guess I opened your window a mite rough."

"Thank you," she said slowly, "for clearing the air in here." A gamine smile quirked her lips. "I'd best get upstairs now, out of this draft."

As the three waddies trudged out to get the trunks off the wagon, Latigo Doyle remarked in slightly awed tones, "It's hard to tell who's got the most problems to worry about—a man that big jigger looks mean at, or a gal he smiles at!"

★

Chapter 3

The trunks were upstairs by the time Curly Bub Becasse and Shukka came to. Curly Bub started cursing with his first conscious breath, but shut up when Voight threatened to stuff his revolver down his throat. Shukka, his jaw swollen as if he were trying to swallow a lemon, glared balefully, but limped out of the house without argument.

"The wagon'll come in handy," Voight said. "We gotta take them corpses out of here before the gal stirs her stumps, and haul 'em to Doc Lozier so he can start finding what cashed 'em in."

Working swiftly, they packed the bodies into the wagonbed and covered them with tarpaulins. Curly Bub griped and muttered, but grudgingly agreed to obey Voight's orders. Shukka's eyes were like burning coals as he mounted the seat beside Becasse, tight-lipped and mum.

"A corpse cart! I question how legal this is," Ingersoll complained querulously, perusing the tarp-covered bodies. "I can't afford trouble with authorities. Besides, I've an interest in this property, and feel I should be consulted about what's to be done."

"I'm the authority hearabouts right now," Deputy Voight growled, "and if anyone gets called on the carpet, it'll be me. Just spur your bronc and go back to town, Thaddeus; there ain't nothing you can do here till Yokum shows up."

Jessie turned to the waddies. "Did I hear you say you were looking for a job of riding?" she asked. "Looks to me like you've got jobs right here. This spread needs hands, and McQuade's niece shouldn't be left alone."

"But what about McQuade?" Hicks asked. "He mightn't like it—or us."

"I don't figure Yokum McQuade will offer much objection when—*if*—he shows up," Ki responded quietly.

Voight gave him a startled glance. "You think something's happened to Yokum?" he asked in a low voice.

"I can't say for certain," Ki murmured, glancing at the wagon. Becasse was gathering up his reins and growling at Ingersoll, who had mounted and pulled alongside the front wheel, still muttering indignantly. "Suppose you walk over to the stable with me."

Voight fell in step with Ki, who told him, "We're sure there're marks of five glasses on the table, the prints of five pairs of shoes in the dust under the table. Five men sat down there last night; four stayed seated."

"You mean Yokum—?"

"I mean nothing, yet," Ki interrupted. Reaching the stable he did not immediately secure their horses' rigs. Instead, he led the deputy into one stall after another, pointing to the feed boxes each in turn. After the fifth row he paused, "D'you see? Five horses besides our two ate in this row of stalls last night. No horses here now. And it's certain those four didn't walk to get here."

Voight swore under his breath. "This's gettin' too topsy-turvey for me," he declared. "Let's be ske-daddlin' back to town."

Soon the deputy, Jessie, and Ki were mounting up in the yard. Nearby, the waddies were coin-tossing to see who went and fetched their warbags from town. About then the girl came outside, bundled in dry clothes, coat, and boots. "I'm more grateful than I can say, for all your kindness to a perfect stranger," she told them earnestly. She centered on Ki. "I really don't know how to thank you, Mr.—?"

Ki gave his name and introduced Jessie and Deputy Voight.

"I'm Elizabeth Wyndam," she told them. "Yokum McQuade is my mother's brother. I've never seen him, but when she died a few months ago, he wrote and invited me to make my home here. I can't understand why he wasn't there to meet me, but pray it doesn't mean worse. I know nothing of ranch life."

"I'm sure there's a good reason and we'll know shortly," Jessie said, and exchanged quick glances with Ki before going on. "We'll drop by tomorrow and see how things are managing. If I'm tied up, Ki will come for sure."

Ki nodded. "Just ask the boys here for anything

you want done. They rode out here to work for your uncle, now that the busy time is here. Real busy." He looked meaningfully at each of the waddies, who immediately understood.

As they were riding out of the yard, the wagon ahead of them was lurching out of sight through the mists. Thaddeus Ingersoll's mackintosh-flapping figure could be made out, hunched in his saddle, his bent back almost visibly oozing resentment.

"Ol' Squeaky Clean doesn't take kindly to meddling in his pastures," Voight remarked, chuckling. "He's okay, and quite a few ladies think he's an attractive package. But he drives a tight bargain. Yokum better pay up, or Ingersoll will slap a foreclosure on his spread, sure as shootin'. And I dunno what'll become of Miz Elizabeth if Yokum don't happen to show hisself."

Somehow Jessie couldn't get overly worried. She'd seen Becasse leer and the girlish Miss Wyndam storm up into a spitfire woman, only to simmer down, sultry-coy, around Ki. And to change so naturally, so sincerely, that men like Voight would fret and care for her—now, that took talent. Jessie respected it, the strength and will it reflected, and suspected Elizabeth would manage to land on her feet no matter the fall. Elizabeth was a survivor.

"How long a trip to Unity?" Jessie asked.

"Take the darn wagon about four hours," Voight replied. "A good horse can make it in two. We turn off about a mile farther on, and nope, we don't take the Lechuza at all. Take the bottom fork of this track. The Lechuza makes a business of *not* running through towns!"

A margin of less than four hours had passed, however, when the horsemen and the wagon pulled in by a small building with a doctor's shingle swining in front of it. They deposited the tarpaulin-shrouded corpses in the examination office, under the watchful guidance of Doc Lozier.

About the same age as Voight, Lozier had a double chin, wore steel-rimmed spectacles, and smoked a smelly cigar. He listened to Jessie and Ki's story with many grunts, and when it was finished, he was given an inquiring glance by the deputy. It was apparent that Voight relied on the judgment as well as the friendship of the doctor.

"I'll perform an autopsy and see what I can find out," Doc Lozier said without much confidence. "Looks like poison of some sort to me. Maybe the hellions just drank themselves to death, though. You know any of 'em, Quentin? I never saw 'em before."

Deputy Voight shook his head. "Well, I better start inquiries about Yokum and see if anybody knows where he went," he said, and departed accompanied by Jessie and Ki.

They rode back up the main street. The drizzle had stopped, the clouds gone over and past, and roofs were steaming in the afternoon sun. It would take a while, though, for the street to dry hard again; its mud surface squished and gulped underhoof. Midway along the second block, Voight reined in by his law office, a squat sheriff's substation squeezed between a mercantile and a feed store.

"Stay handy. Doc Lozier holds inquests when he's a mind to," the deputy advised. Answering a casual question from Jessie, he replied, "Telegraph office? Sure, in Trader Lane, 'round the next corner, aside the building with the stage depot." He glanced wonderingly at Jessie, then at Ki, but they vouchsafed no explanation.

A few minutes later they entered the telegraph office. There Jessie concocted a carefully worded message which she ordered sent to Frank Manglesdorf, at her Starbuck import-export company in San Francisco. She could have cabled Starbuck headquarters at her ranch, which had the staff and sources to handle anything, but wire service this far from Texas could take days. And since her query had to do with out here, the Far West region, she reckoned the answer might be easier as well as faster to get out here. If anybody could, chances were it'd be Manglesdorf. He was chief of security at the company, a shrewd, old-line operative with myriad connections and a retentive memory.

"I'll check back for the reply," she told the telegrapher.

They went back up Trader Lane, which cut alley-wide between two sizable buildings. At Main Street, they remounted and plowed through the mud to the livery, where they stabled their tuckered horses.

The hostler was a ribald geezer, who gave them a rheumy-eyed once-over and then opined, "A young married couple, ain'tcha? If thar's one thing I admire, it's a young married couple."

"We're not married, I'll have you know," Jessie spat.

"Just skylarking, hey?" He cackled. "I admire that even more."

Jessie looked at the hostler with mayhem in her cold green eyes. Hastily, Ki changed topics. Hoping to learn something of local matters, he asked, "Much

30

going on in these parts? I mean, anybody hiring here-abouts, you think?"

The hostler rubbed his jaw. "Nope, nobody's hired a cook in ages."

"I don't cook. I don't do housekeeping, either," Ki retorted. "Come on, now, do you know or don't you?"

"Wal . . . maybe one job, paying fifty an' found."

"Fifty and found!" Ki shook his head. "I doubt any outfit pays more than thirty and found these days. Who's loco enough to pay fifty?"

"Suicide Spread."

"Suicide Spread? There's no such iron ever been!" Jessie snapped testily, figuring the hostler was just out to yank Ki's chain, and she started stalking off. "Forget we even asked!"

The hostler thought that funnier yet, and slapped his knee hooting.

They ate at a nearby cafe, then, and moseyed about the town of Unity, namesake of Unity Valley. Very soon they decided it didn't look like a bad town, a really dangerous town, but bad towns rarely did.

Main Street was wide enough on either side for three wagons abreast, and seemed to be at least six blocks long. It was a good thing it was fairly sizable for, as they soon learned, Unity was the hub of a thriving, comfortably settled ranching district. There was a constant flow of traffic, shuttling to and fro and churning Main Street into a gumbo badlands.

The shops, houses, and offices that lined both sides of the street were decent enough, but they had to share boardwalk frontage with double the normal number of saloons, some of them pretty squalid. The usual loafers in doorways and by hitching racks had more than the average sprinkling of hardcase gunwolves. And Jessie and Ki knew a hardcase when they saw one, whether dressed in respectable gambler's black or rooty-tooty woolly chaps.

"The Lechuza Trail may skip this town," Jessie commented grimly, "but the lobos taking it sure know where to turn off. . . ."

The man in Trader Lane was a mongrel too, but a different sort of mongrel. When they checked back for replies, he was across from the telegraph office, pausing to light a brown-paper cigarette. Snoutfaced, shaggy-haired, in faded blues and a brush coat, he looked like a sorry chuckline cowpoke, except for his well-kept pistol rig. Tossing the match aside, he glanced up at them with flat indifference, then headed down-lane.

One mean cur, Jessie sensed. He wasn't a gunslinger, not with his pistol worn hip high, backwoods style. Nor was he common riffraff, harmless and dirty as a livery stable loafer. But another sort of riffraff was dirty dangerous, raring to fight anyone, over anything, anytime, place and way they could maim or slay. You didn't have to be a hired gun to be a killer.

The man went in the next door down. A sign above the door said GRUMBECK SONS' COOPERAGE; the workshop ran facing the telegraph office. Jessie glanced at Ki, who seemed not to've given the man any thought at all. He was perusing the alley as though he'd dropped something.

There was a reply waiting at the telegraph office. The operator eyed Jessie with warm interest as he handed her the message, but would've burned with curiosity if he could've read it correctly.

CORONADO MINE LOCHINVAR ROBBED THREE DAYS AGO GOLD INGOTS VALUED APPROXIMATELY ONE HUNDRED THOUSAND DOLLARS STOP DRIVER TWO GUARDS KILLED STOP NO WITNESSES ALIVE TO IDENTIFY CULPRITS STOP SHIPMENT SUPPOSED SECRET STOP DRIFT FOREMAN MAYHEW KNAUB MISSING FROM WORK STOP HEAVY SET BLUE EYES DARK HAIR SHOT WITH GRAY STOP F M

After Ki read it, Jessie noted low-voiced, "Hundred thousand worth is a heavy wad of gold— almost four hundred pounds. I imagine four strong horses could pack it all, though, and riders."

"One man alone would still need four horses, Jessie, plus one to ride. And it seems that Yokum McQuade was pressed for ready cash." Pausing, frowning thoughtfully, Ki then said, "I wonder if we can go out a back way."

"Why?"

"There might be trash blocking the front."

The operator took five dollars of persuasion to grudgingly agree. "Okay, but it don't make sense. The rear exit just opens onto the lane again."

They followed him through a door behind the counter, down a passage, past a cubby with an unmade bed. Just beyond this little room was another door on the opposite side of the passage. The operator unbolted it and they stepped into the lane, Ki leading with a cautious, watchful stalk. He suspected an ambush, and found one.

Scarely spitting distance up-lane, on this side of the entrance to Grumbech Sons' Cooperage, two men stood concealed behind a stack of barrels. They held revolvers at the ready; one, in ragged denim, was peering around the stack at the telegraph office door, while the other, in old army clothes, was pressing against the wall.

Suddenly, then, so many things happened so quick that Jessie was never able later to put them together in a picture that satisfied her. Instead of closing the back door, the curious operator took a gander, his voice, startled and confused, bawling *"A guntrap!"* The two ambushers turned, firing wildly, the siding on Jessie's left exploding into flying splinters.

She dove to the lane's boardwalk, rolling, as Ki sprang aside and snapped off a *shuriken*. Later, she remembered hearing the operator scream, then the *thwack* as Ki's spinning steel disk buried itself in solid bone. The man in army clothes slumped erratically just as she twisted about, triggering her pistol. She missed by a hair the man in denim, who was jostled by his falling, *shuriken*-struck partner. He froze, horrified. Deadly vicious when hiding behind cover, he was now actually facing gunfire, and his backbone seemed to melt. Bawling "Don't shoot!" he tore off at a lope, taking a chance that no one would blast him from the rear.

No one did, for the door to the cooperage shop wrenched open just then, and a third ambusher came tearing out. He looked like he had when Ki last saw him, like a sorry chuckline cowhand with a well-kept pistol—which was now bucking in his hand, a rapid hail of lead tunneling down the lane. The ambusher running away gave a yelp and a veering lurch, avoiding being hit as he frantically plunged by the third ambusher and on up the lane.

A whirring *shuriken* pierced the third ambusher and he went down, still firing as he started dragging himself forward. A slug from Jessie's pistol caught him, its impact tugging a moan from him and slamming his face into the boards. He started raising himself, pointing his smoking revolver, beyond feeling or caring anymore, existing solely on feral hatred as he vainly tried to line his next shot. But already from Ki's hand a *shuriken* soared, striking ahead of another bullet fired by Jessie. The third ambusher crumpled, gushing blood, his neck skewered and jugular veins severed.

Ki yelled "Stay here!" at Jessie and sprinted forward, leaping over the bodies. Ahead, at the mouth of the lane, the fleeing ambusher cut onto Main Street, vanishing from view. Ki chased after, reaching the mouth—and colliding hard with three strangers striding along the street.

The impact knocked the nearest—a bearded, raw-boned bruiser—off balance and into his two companions, a scar-faced 'breed and a solid, stocky blond. These three were range-clad like working cowpunchers, and they all cursed irately, fury rushing into their eyes.

Ki, rocked to his heels, came up against the corner of the lane. He caught himself, grinned tightly at the man, and murmured "Sorry" as he moved on in pursuit of the fleeing ambusher.

The bearded man lunged, threw out a thick arm and checked Ki. "Not yet, but you gonna be!" he snarled, exhaling the rank stench of rotgut whiskey, goaded on by the other two, who were shouting encouragement.

"Yah, he can't go shovin' us aroun'!"

"L'arn him who's ramrod, Wahoo!"

The brute called Wahoo punched out wickedly at Ki's face. Ki swayed aside, and the callused, gnarled fist whizzed over his shoulder. Almost at the same instant, something like the business end of a sledge hammer took Wahoo squarely on the angle of his jutting chin. Wahoo lifted from his feet and landed on the boardwalk, knocked breathless.

Swearing luridly, the other two clawed for their holstered pistols as Ki launched at them over the downed Wahoo, intent on catching up with the escaping ambusher. They were still drawing when Ki's shoulder struck the blond man and spun him to the edge of the boardwalk, teetering above the mud, his arms gyrating.

"Grab him!" Ki yelled, shoving the 'breed, as the latter attempted to keep the blond from falling. Ki jumped back against the building as a great geyser of mud marked the entrance of the two men into its depth.

Now the ambusher was gone, however, lost somewhere beyond the gathering throng that had been attracted by the shots. Stymied, angered by the stupid delay, Ki turned to go back, only to confront an enraged Wahoo rearing upright.

"I'd plug yuh, 'cept yuh're unarmed," Wahoo roared, wielding his revolver like a club. "So I'll only pistolwhip yuh to a yaller pulp instead!"

Wahoo swung fast, but Ki was faster. Before his revolver could connect, a *mae-geri-keage* snap-kick

36

pistoned into Wahoo's solar plexus. There was an eruption of breath, and Wahoo crashed to his knees with a ragged gasp of agony, clutching his belly.

"Better call it a day, Wahoo," a gruff voice ordered. Ki swiveled to see the crowd parting, Deputy Voight and Jessie hastening through to the front.

In their wake came steaming the portly banker, Thaddeus Ingersoll, who yelled vindictively, "Now will you act, Voight? That woman with you and her accomplice are menaces to any community. Arrest them, I say!"

"On what charge, Thaddeus?" Voight asked mildly.

"What charge!" Ingersoll gestured at Wahoo who was still kneeling jackknifed, dizzily gasping for air, and at the mud-covered pair climbing back onto the boardwalk. "Murder! Assault! They've picked our law-abiding community to do their feudin' in!"

"Murder nothin'!" Voight snapped. "And odds are here that the Block-P boys were pickin' on Ki, 'cept for once their usual bullying backfired."

"What little we may've done was in self-defense," Jessie stated firmly. "We're carrying no quarrel with anyone."

Ki nodded, leaning toward Ingersoll and stage-whispering conspiratorially, "Tell you the truth, from what I could make of it here, everyone slipped."

"Aw'ri', you," Ingersoll growled, gnashing teeth, "you're the root of enough trouble, see, without cracking wise with more."

"You ask this Wahoo fellow. You ask him if he didn't slip."

A man hidden in the crowd gave out a loud horse-laugh.

37

Wahoo panted, "I slipped, like he says." His unexpected admission surprised everyone, including Ki, who turned, frowning, to see a bystander gripping the woozy man by the elbow, helping him up. Close by stood the other two Block-P boys, spitting and cussing, attempting to scrape the mud from their faces and eyes.

Ingersoll began sputtering, "N-now listen, Wahoo—"

"I slipped, we all slipped, an' don't nobody forget it!"

"Then that's that," Voight declared, nodding. "You listen to y'self if'n you like, Thaddeus, but I got work a-waitin' to do."

Jessie and Ki left with the deputy. Just before the corner of the lane, Jessie felt the impulse to glance back. With Ingersoll stood the trio, one sucking in air, two wiping muck from their faces with bandannas, all four of them staring after Ki. Staring with looks fit to kill.

Voight elbowed a path through the swelling mob, down Trader Lane to the morbid group collected around the grisly, bloodied corpses. "Rupe and Seth, the Furrow cousins," he informed Jessie and Ki. "More'n likely it was Seth's brother, Nate, who lammed out. They've a hardscrabble ranch up in the hills and raise a few cows, but're suspected of mainly living off a li'l rustling and a li'l third-rate gunplay."

"For anyone in particular?" Jessie asked.

"Nope. The Furrows weren't particular about nothin'." Voight then went over to the telegraph operator, who lay sprawled outside the rear door with half the crown of his head shot off. "Poor Ogilvy. He never did have much luck. What in blazes d'you suppose the Furrows was bent on?"

"Fracas and mayhem," Ki said somberly, as though that answered it. "And where's it gotten them?"

"Boot Hill," Voight offered, and turned to the crowd. "Some of you rubberneckers haul these guys over to the undertaker's," he ordered, jerking a thumb at the bodies. Then he said to Jessie, "Doc Lozier oughta be told. Suppose we drop in and see what he found out about them four dead'uns we delivered. . . ."

They found the doctor at his office desk. When they told him of the latest crop of corpses, his comments were sulphurous, and were followed by a disgusted snort at Deputy Voight's question.

"A poison of some type," he declared. "Nothing I know or ever heard tell of, apart from old-timey rumors about Injun poisons. 'Pears to be alkaloid in nature, sort of like you'd get from a bad mushroom —for instance, the Deadly Amanita, but not quite the same."

"I thought such poison caused violent convulsions," Jessie said.

Doc Lozier nodded. "That's what stumps me. From what y'all tell me, the victims were seated peacefully at a table. Folks suffering convulsions don't die that way. Well, maybe Yokum McQuade can shed some light on the subject when he returns."

"*If* he returns!" Voight grunted.

"What do you mean by that, Quentin?" the doctor asked.

"Well, Ki here showed me that there was five men settin' around the table drinkin'. Four of 'em stayed there, one git up and gat. Now who would that one have been? Yokum had let all his hands go and there weren't nobody left at his ranch house save him. Who but Yokum would've been there late in the evenin', when those four jiggers must've arrived. If Yokum was the fifth one, you wouldn't hardly expect him to come back hereabouts again, would you?"

"But why would Yokum want to poison four gents he never saw before?" demanded Doc Lozier.

Voight shrugged. "How do we know he never saw 'em afore? We don't know everything about Yokum McQuade. He ain't been here over long. . . . Come an' begun his M-Over-Y spread just a year afore Thad Ingersoll took over the bank, and Ingersoll's been here less'n two years."

"That reminds me . . ." Doc Lozier called to an urchin who was dangling his legs from a chair in the outer office. "C'mere, son. Here's Mist' Ingersoll's sleeping powders. Take 'em over to him."

The boy hurried off.

"Ingersoll takes enough of that stuff nightly to conk a horse out," Doc Lozier explained. "I was just finishing the prescription when you came in. If Ingersoll wasn't always cudgeling his brains over how to make an extra dollar, maybe he'd sleep better of nights."

"He's wringy tight, okay," Voight allowed, "but he sure put the bank back on its legs, after ol' John Tighe almost sunk it from easy-goin' loans."

"Nothing easy-going about Thaddeus Ingersoll."

"No, Doc, there ain't," Voight admitted with a

worried air. "He'll be foreclosin' on the M-Over-Y if Yokum don't make payment pronto. There's plenty of steers on the spread to take care of it, too, or I'm a heap mistook."

"Sounds like it better be done," Ki said then. "I'll see that a gather gets started, as soon as I ride out there tomorrow morning."

"You'll have a mite of a chore, combin' 'em critters out of the brakes an' gittin' 'em rounded up in time. Hicks an' Grampus an' Latigo Doyle are good hands when bossed proper, but they ain't no great shakes at thinkin' on their lonesomes." Abruptly Voight paused, eyeing Ki with agitation. "Whup! What am I saying? You're not planning to stick around these parts, are you?"

"Why not?"

"You whupped Wahoo Delgardo, and dumped two Block-P boys, to boot."

"We had a little set-to, but, well, bygones should be bygones."

"I'd dasn't dream such fancies, if I were you."

Just then the sound of galloping hoofbeats could be heard thundering from the street. Glancing out the office window, they saw Wahoo Delgardo and a number of cowpunchers riding past, heading westerly out of town.

"Headin' home, I reckon," Voight said with a sigh. "Friend, the Block-P has been known to ventilate for less'n you did. Many claim Felix Pierce is the meanest bast—er, *rancher* in the state, with ice for a heart and acid for blood, and a crew hired to match. 'Course, there're others who swear Pierce is a gruff but hon'rable soul—usually they're the ones

41

mortgaged to the bank, Pierce bein' son-in-law of Ingersoll, y'see."

"How convenient," Jessie commented sardonically.

"Oh, Pierce doesn't need Ingersoll's influence. He'd built the biggest ranch around long afore he married Miz Millicent and her pa moved here to bank. Fact is, rustlers have been hitting the Block-P harder than the other, smaller spreads, and recently some of his cattle have been plain shot down and even blown up with stump-blasting powder."

"Well, rustled and slaughtered stock is enough to turn any rancher into a ring-tailed roarer," Ki responded. "But all the same, I'll stay till Miss Starbuck is ready to leave the area."

Voight eyed Jessie hopefully. "Tomorrow, ma'am?"

"No, tomorrow I'll be at the Anvil, visiting Randall Avalon."

Making a face like he'd bitten a green persimmon, Voight croaked, aghast, "Suicide Spread."

"The Anvil? I thought the hostler was funning about Suicide Spread."

"No, ma'am, that's what folks call the Anvil."

"We'd no idea. Is Avalon really paying fifty and found?"

"Well, he's pledging to, but I ain't sure if or for how long he can. His Anvil's a smallish spread west of here, stocked with plump, juicy beef, but it borders on Pierce's in some places. It got tagged Suicide on account of it and the Block-P have a kind of feud 'tween 'em, which, if you consider their sizes, ain't no contest a-tall. It's lost some cattle and had a

42

few men shot up too, but Pierce holds the Anvil's to blame for the rustling and suchlike."

"That doesn't make sense, if they're losing too."

"It does and it doesn't. Could be the Anvil is trying to cover its tracks by claiming rustled stock, and the men it's lost were shot while raiding other ranches. Leastwise that's what Pierce asserts, and face it, his opinion carries weight in these parts. And for a fact, ol' Rawhide Avalon has the only known quantity of blastin' powder outside the general store. He bought a case of it, in one-pound canisters, to level boulders for a new barn, or so he says. He ain't never built no new barn, though he did buy some lumber and hauled it out to his place. He claims some canisters got stolen from him, and Gawd help any bigmouth who questions him different. Rawhide is a cantankerous coot, a lot like his nickname."

"A regular blister, is he?" Jessie smiled wryly. "All the more reason we should go, I'm sure you'd say, but we have to stay anyway for the inquests."

Doc Lozier answered, shaking his head. "No, you won't need to attend any inquests. Deputy Voight can take your depositions, if he ain't already; then he an' I'll open and shut the formalities sometime later. Now in fairness to Rawhide, he ain't exactly what you'd call a diplomat, and Pierce may have the bulge 'cause he's got more money and backing, but Rawhide's friends are the real goods, and his crew'd ride to hell an' gone for him, and that's a lot."

"Still an' all," Voight insisted darkly, "your best bet is to hit the trail out of this country while you can. That's my advice."

"Much obliged," Jessie replied. "I've observed

that once people start to run, they usually keep on running the rest of their lives. I'm too much a lady to be seen to run scared, though. It simply isn't done in proper society."

Voight sighed the sigh of men plagued by women.

Chapter 4

The route Jessie and Ki took out of Unity headed west, toward Rawhide Avalon's Anvil ranch. It had been this Rawhide Avalon who'd telegraphed Jessie in Texas with one terse message:

USE YOUR HELP NOW

The rancher's urgent plea had been sufficient for Jessie to immediately make plans for a trip. A decade before, the Avalon family had given refuge to her father at great personal risk, without question or compensation, saving him from enemies who were hunting him down. Alex Starbuck had never been able to repay their kindness; his every offer of help had been politely but firmly declined, Rawhide refusing to be "beholden." After a brief note from Rawhide saying his wife had sickened and died, little

45

more had been heard for quite some time until his cryptic telegram.

Nothing in the routine reports and field-operative dispatches that poured into Starbuck Enterprises indicated what Rawhide's mysterious trouble might be. Jessie assumed it had to be serious—meaning dangerous—but it didn't matter. Alex Starbuck never forgot a debt or a friend; neither did Jessie. After ten years Rawhide Avalon needed help, and help he would get. With interest.

Now, as they rode along, Jessie remarked, "Surely that ambush was tied in with Rawhide, but I'll be switched if I can figure out how."

"Maybe it wasn't, or only indirectly. I've a hunch it might've had more to do with your telegrams. When we went back, remember, one of the Furrow cousins was lighting a cigarette. He must've waited there for some while, for some reason, for the lane was littered with brown paper cigarette butts."

"That was the trash blocking the front, was it?"

"That, and the gun-trash smoking them. A trap made more sense than mere coincidence when the telegrapher took our five bucks, showing he could've been bribed to spill information. We needed someone to talk, though, but instead of nabbing the only one alive, I had to go tangle with the Block-P."

For that matter, there was a chance of another run-in with the Block-P boys, who had ridden off in this direction as well. Once beyond the town limits, Jessie and Ki kept on the lookout while memorizing the lay of the land: a motte of timber to right of them, a long draw to the south, and yonder a coulee in which a regiment could have been hidden.

After perhaps two hours they reached the western

46

foothills. Darkness had come, a cloud-shrouded full moon piercing through every so often, bathing the terrain in phosphorescent glow for a moment, before falling eclipsed once again in banks of deep gloom. The trail climbed by gradual rises through woods and fields, eventually dipping into a wide basin of pasturage and wooded stands.

They had seen nothing calculated to alarm, but Jessie drew rein now to listen. She had a fair notion they were on Felix Pierce's Block-P range, and she knew they were still aimed on the right course. Yet they had not spotted anything or anybody from the time they'd started out—not one sign, at any rate, which would indicate that they were tagging the Block-P crew. And they should have by now.

Ki pulled up his mount and set himself to sense more acutely the danger Jessie somehow perceived. Motionless as bronze, they listened. By now it was fully dark—a good time, if a man were of a mind, to inflict damage to an enemy or to avenge real or fancied wrongs. Yet the most they could make of it was a speculation that Wahoo Delgardo and his men had turned off somewhere—and that caused them to ponder if possibly the reason was to divert suspicion; to make it appear as if the crew had dutifully returned to the Block-P ranch for the night, in case news of some disaster might, in a day or so, reach town.

Frustrated, they moved on more cautiously than ever, trying to stay within the concealing verge of a lodgepole-pine forest that more or less bordered the basin. Beyond, the serrated ramparts of the mountains were black. A wind, rising, murmured among the pines and then died. After about another mile, they topped a rise and spied, all at once, a darker

47

patch ahead—and they felt, more than actually perceived, that it was the figure of a man.

The man was moving forward, away from them, with the slithering stealth of an indian. Immediately they checked their horses, dismounting quietly, Jessie loosening her pistol in its holster. But the figure had vanished.

With their left hands through the reins, they led their horses forward a few paces and tethered them to trees, then proceeded stealthily ahead on foot. They were close to the timber's edge, beyond which they could dimly perceive a stretch of grazeland. All over this part of the range they could see dark blots which they immediately recognized as cattle. The scene was serene, but it was, they felt, the silence before a storm.

And as if to support their belief, the sense of jeopardy appeared to be affecting the nearest bunch of cattle. The animals were growing restless; one after another they rose and wandered off, as if driven by some invisible force. Jessie and Ki were now certain that they were not alone here, that the man they'd spotted was but one of the number concealed somewhere near the center of the shifting cattle, some several hundred feet to their right.

Then, as they inched forward on hands and knees, they abruptly beheld a moving figure, high-humped. For a space of a heartbeat the thing looked like nothing human—and it was not. It was a horse, saddled but riderless, that emerged from the trees. At a trot the horse was across the pasture and among the cattle, and quickly faded across the basin.

On the chance that some other prowler might have let his mount stray in that direction, they made haste back to their own horses. It was a fortunate move. Ki had barely reached his black when its ears pricked forward; it seemed to be hearing something, and was preparing to whicker in response to what, Ki reasoned, must be the sensed presence of another animal nearby. Just in time he gripped the horse by its nose, preventing its whinny. Then, with Jessie laying her hand across the mouth of her horse, they led their mounts some little distance into the timber, where again they halted, standing very still.

A twig snapped, over on their right. They crouched, Jessie's hand on her pistol, turning to see a second horse, saddled but riderless, moving at a dead run through the cattle. Something had spooked it, or it had been cut hard with a quirt. Saddled horses did not run for any considerable distance without good cause, they knew. They smothered their own horses' eager whickers with their hands.

They wanted to get away, yet another part of their minds wanted to stick around and discover what was going on. They debated, whispering, over which to do, when the choice was answered for them, from just ahead, out of the darkness.

There was a movement among the cattle, the sound of which was becoming a rumble and then a roar. They saw that by increasing numbers the cows were trundling off toward the shadowed hills on the far side of the basin. Then, all at once, they heard voices—downwind the mutter reached them in a sing-song grumble against the curtain of the night. It swiftly became distinct enough for them to tell that the voices were coming from a number of men passing through the timber. Abruptly a single figure stood etched against the night sky in sable silhouette.

And then the dark was split asunder with a blazing glare and a deafening explosion. The earth-shaking blast was followed by the frenzied bawl of cattle bolting, stampeding about them. Their horses reared, panic-stricken, and would have bolted had not Jessie and Ki clung to the bridles. For ten, fifteen seconds they were in the midst of a deadly tornado of hoofs and horns, and then they finally succeeded in quieting their skittish horses, while the cattle thundered off in every direction. They hoped, and believed, that in all the chaos they were still undetected by the hidden men who'd set off the black powder charge.

For black powder was what it had been. A foolishly expensive way to slaughter livestock, Jessie thought, since even a large blast would kill only a relatively small proportion of the herd, whereas bullets would have been much more effective.

They were mounting their nervous horses, preparing to ride, when suddenly they heard voices again, blurred by distance. The sound came to them in a faint mutter, the words indistinguishable. But it was enough to convince them that whoever had set off the explosion had plenty of backup support—and would make it fatal for them if they should be caught.

Indeed, six men abruptly rode at a gallop from the timber, racing off in the direction taken by the riderless horses. None of the six was riding double, though, which made Jessie and Ki wonder what had become of the owners of the missing steeds. Cautiously they jogged toward the open area of the basin, aware it would be an easy matter for hidden sharpshooters to pick them off. . . . The moonlit darkness formed each tree and bush into an armed marksman, lurking, taking aim. . . .

The stillness held. Away from the wooded fringe they found the carcasses of several steers that had been destroyed by the explosion. Farther on, at sight of numerous small objects scattered about, they dismounted and examined the ground for a radius of many yards. They retrieved some bits of clothing, and spotted fragments of flesh and bone. Just as they were thinking to quit their search, Jessie glimpsed a stubby gray-black cannister on the ground.

"Black powder," she noted, picking it up and showing Ki.

According to its label, the can held one pound of Marsten 2XX, suitable for hard rock, ores, stumps, ice, and submarine blasting. The pried-up lid was slightly open, and a length of double-tape fuse was inserted in the powder; the other end of the fuse was charred, as though it had lighted poorly and burned out.

About then the moon faded behind clouds again. Nothing could be gained by waiting around, they figured, and after Jessie packed the cannister in her saddlebag, they rode back the way they had come, through the timber to the trail.

They were just starting to emerge from the wooded fringe when they saw three horsemen heading towards them across the basin. Hastily they ducked back under cover, spurring their horses sidewards and threading between the trees at a quickening trot. It didn't appear that the oncoming riders were pursuing them, or even that they were aware of them, but at last look, through the screen of trees and brush, the three had grown in number to five riders . . . and all kept coming.

Jessie and Ki urged their horses on up into the

hills that loomed beyond the flanking timber. For more than an hour they forged between bouldered outcroppings and through scrubby thickets, trying to maintain a westerly course in line with the trail. In time they intersected a path, an easily overlooked path, no more than a single-file ribbon where passing hoofs had beaten the ground raw. Yet it wound more or less in their direction, and was better than the fresh trail they were blazing, so they decided to try it awhile.

Presently the path joined a larger wagon trail, which they assumed was the same trail they'd taken from town. Despite the increased risk of discovery, they turned onto the trail and loped westward along its wandering course. As far as they could tell, there was no sigh of humans, friendly or otherwise, and they were fairly confident of having distanced themselves enough from the scene of the explosion to be free of any immediate suspicion.

After a long stretch, they came upon a narrow lane that cut away to the right. Nailed to a peeled log beside the lane, was a large wooden signboard carved with the Anvil brand and the name AVALON.

Angling onto the lane, they curved through a grove and reached an open field. Almost immediately two riders appeared, one erupting out of a slash, the other hammering down a hillside, and converging on them. Both were husky, hard-featured, saddle-worn waddies, packing handguns and carrying Winchesters in saddle boots.

One of the cowhands said, "You're on private property."

"We're heading for the house," Jessie replied.

"Mist' Avalon will have retired, ma'am."

"Then we'll have to awaken him. He's expecting us."

"Well . . ." He looked dubious. "We'll just ride along with y'all."

The cowhands didn't ride beside them; they rode slightly behind them.

The lane snaked on across rocky knolls and rough breaks, but increasingly the landscape consisted of pocket meadows dotted with cattle. Soon, across a grassy field, Jessie and Ki saw a line of cottonwoods, indicating a creek. It was another fifteen minutes before they spotted the ranch proper, fronting that creek. There was a big barn, bunkhouse, cookshack and mess, smithy shop, and several corrals grouped around the main house, all dark and silent when they pulled up in the ranchyard.

Hitching their horses at posts by the main house, they stepped to the porch, and the cowhand who'd spoken rapped the brass knocker on the front door. After a moment the door swung inward. A burly old man with white Dunrearie whiskers furring his weathered face padded out barefoot, wearing a red flannel nightshirt and brandishing a candle. He eyed his visitors uncordially.

"Sorry to pester, Mr. Avalon," the man said, "but we latched onto these folks coming in from the trail, and they claim you're expecting them."

"Bullsh—" Avalon began. Then he choked off and peered closer, and grinned with welcoming recognition. "Jessica Starbuck—and Ki, by God! C'mon in!"

Entering, they were ushered into the parlor. Rawhide Avalon hastily lit a lamp, gabbing in a loud, excited voice. That aroused a fat, middle-aged woman, who shuffled in and was introduced as Bertha, his housekeeper and cook. Bertha promptly declared a snack was in order and assaulted the kitchen with a frenzy. The unusual activity awoke the day crew from their snorings in the bunkhouse, and within minutes a tall, muscular man rushed in, bare-chested, hitching his jeans with one hand and grip-ping a pistol in the other, demanding to know what the middle-of-the-night crisis was about.

"Meet my *segundo,* Long Tom Hughes," Avalon said. Greetings were exchanged, more lamps were lit, and Jessie gave the foreman more than one glance. Thirtyish, tanned, fine-featured, thoughtful of lip, and level-gazed, Long Tom Hughes looked all cattleman to Jessie, with emphasis on the man.

"We're a mite touchy here, as you can see," Raw-hide explained, as Hughes laid his pistol aside. "You'll find that the Block-P harasses me and my boys and my cows every chance they can without getting caught. And Long Tom had an idea that they'd be up to skulduggery tonight."

"More'n an idea," Hughes said, nodding. "Any evening Wahoo rounds up his crew in town, we get stock lifted or butchered, water holes fouled, get shot at or some such devilment. When the supply wagon got back this afternoon with word of Block-P pack-ing the Esquire Saloon, I figured they was planning to pay us a late-night visit. Only, well, you turned out to be our visitors."

"If the Block-P would only leave us in peace, we'd do fine, but they won't," Rawhide growled. "We can fight, and will. But we don't have the wherewithal to win, Jessie, and I won't have my boys massacreed for no lost causes. If Starbuck can pin Felix Pierce's ears back even a little bit I'd be eternally grateful."

"Well, we'll do what we can," Jessie assured him.

Long Tom Hughes reared, perplexed. "You brought *them* to—"

"Yep, at my special invite. I want you to help them all you can and give them the same trust you do me."

For a moment Hughes seemed to struggle with his tongue. Then coldly he said, "No disrespect intended, Mr. Avalon, but what the tunket's gotten into you? Why, they're total strangers!"

"Not hardly. In any event, I'm willing to take whatever risk there is. If I'm wrong, nothing's the worser, 'cause we're licked the way we're going."

Bertha summoned them to the dining room for a "snack" that would've ruined many a restaurant. Rawhide Avalon spoke garrulously, but Long Tom Hughes spurned the talk and the company. Piqued, Jessie wondered if there mightn't be more behind the foreman's animosity than mere mistrust of outsiders. The thought came to her that perhaps Hughes and some Anvil crewmen were the riders she'd seen galloping away, right after the explosion that destroyed Block-P cattle. Certainly they'd know the quickest way back here, and could've arrived long before her and Ki. If so, then she sure was glad she hadn't let slip, and they hadn't chanced to find, the cannister in her bags.

Of course this was sheer speculation on her part. But by the same stroke, as much as she liked Rawhide and tended to believe him and his foreman, she mustn't allow her feelings to prejudice her judgment. She and Ki had to tread carefully, after all, for if it turned out that the Anvil was truly behind the blasting and rustling troubles . . .

The ranch could well become their own Suicide Spread.

★
Chapter 5

The Anvil bunkhouse was a resonant black cave of grumblings and snores. Ki slept through the racket undisturbed, rousing with the crew at dawn, and riding out after breakfast for Yokum McQuade's ranch.

When Ki reached the M-Over-Y, he found Elizabeth Wyndam out back of the house, scrubbing a castiron skillet vigorously with lava grit and lye soap. She wore a striped calico wrapper and a bib apron left by the ex-cook, and she wore them like a grape wears its skin. No mistaking her now for a growing girl, Ki saw appreciatively; although youthfully trim and wasp-waisted, this gal had the succulent breasts and ripened thighs of a grown woman.

She welcomed him cheerily, asking, "Any news of my uncle?"

"Afraid not, Miss Wyndam—"

"Call me Beth," she said, disappointed but trying not to show it.

"Beth." Briefly, then, Ki sketched the situation for her, about the roundup, implying a forced cattle sale to pay a loan was standard routine.

She listened attentively, looking at him in a different sort of manner. Not hard exactly but carefully. As though she were buying a piece of yard goods.

"Do what you think's best," she responded stiffly. "You will anyway. I know you're fooling me, and yet I trust you."

"You know I'm fooling you, and yet you trust me."

"Yes. Raising money and all that is true, I'm sure, but there's more to it. Something more important you're skirting over, keeping from me."

Ki, looking baffled, shook his head. "Your guess is good as mine."

"Listen," Beth said, her voice sharpening, "I'm a female. Time and again from my father on, I've heard you two-faced fibbers say, 'never tell a female anything seriously important.' I've a feel for men—" She flushed, faltering. "My, that came out wrong, didn't it?"

"When we get hysterical," he said kindly, "sometimes we don't know what we're saying."

"I never get hysterical!"

"That's fine," Ki said. He patted Beth on the top of the head, as though she were a small boy, and headed off in search of the crew. He had her in a fuming snit now, like he wanted her. Miss Wyndam had a bad time coming up.

Ki found Orville Hicks, Jud Grampus, and Latigo Doyle puttering about the stable and corral, obviously waiting for somebody to give them orders. They got them, in a hurry.

"Gather a shipping herd together for shipment, pronto," Ki directed. "Otherwise that shylock banker will set his hands on the M-Over-Y. Can't wait for Yokum McQuade to show up. Miss Wyndam is boss while he's away, and she's stringing along with what I suggest."

The hands didn't cotton to the job over much, and started out bellyaching a-plenty. As Ki had suspected, there were enough saleable beeves to clear the loan and then some, but it was one mean task to round them up. They were badly scattered and, with the natural contrariness of windies, had sought out the most inaccessible brakes and canyons to hole up in.

"Whoever named that sort of critters 'windies' sure had the right notion," Latigo Doyle groused, after a long chase of a belligerent stray. "I sure am plumb winded."

For all their begrudgings, Doyle and his pards were nonetheless skilled, seasoned cowpunchers. Once they discovered that Ki was always there, driving himself harder than he was them, they made the best of it. Proving from here on in to be willin', untirin', sort of self-humored moanin' an' pissin' workers.

Autumn twilight, soft purple and dusty, clouded the range when they returned to the ranchyard, and golden lamplight gave the main house a sleepy charm. For supper Beth served some sort of thick-sauced stew, filled with lumps of meat, soupy hash potatoes, and hard pancake bread. Ki wondered what the meat was, and decided he was better off if he didn't know.

"I'm not used to such cooking," Beth said. "Sorry it's no better."

"It couldn't be better," Grampus declared, the others grunting agreement as they set to devouring the meal, then second helpings. Food was food.

After supper, the crew had a stint of chores left to do. Ki rode out to check on the small herd they'd gathered that day, and to scout around some just in case the dusk wasn't as peaceful as it seemed. It was almost night now, and a pearlescent full moon was coming to light over the eastern hills. The scrub on the dim canyon floors became an icy blue, although details remained murky, tricky to discern. Ki found he was straining to see, peering harder now than he had earlier in the day, when he'd combed for cows at the same time he'd been scrutinizing the land they'd covered, hunting for the signs and clues he felt confident were there to be found.

"Couldn't have moved that four hundred pounds of bar gold very far, or I'm dead wrong," he thought aloud, halting atop a rimrock to watch and listen. "It's holed up somewhere on this spread, waiting for a chance to be sneaked out. The only holdback, I reckon, is that clear sky full of moon. First quarter-moon or overcast, stormy night, that gold will grow legs. . . ."

Ki rode a cautious circuit back to the ranchyard. Stabling his horse, then, he went and sat in with the crew on a long bench in front of the bunkhouse. The night was growing chilly—except around the bunkhouse bench, where hot air gusted in tornado strength. Relaxing, done for the day, the garrulous waddies were blustering with windy boasts and windier yarns, when they weren't blowing hot gossip and privy rumors.

Ki wasn't there too long, though, before Orville Hicks told him, "The boss wants you." Hicks sat on the other end of the bench, at a vantage for seeing the rear of the house, which was where he was pointing. "Yonder."

Ki turned.

Beth Wyndam was standing at the rear door, backlit by a fan-spread of light from the kitchen, beckoning to him.

Ki said, "Excuse me, gentlemen," and got up, and went to her.

Waiting, smiling faintly, Beth stood with the lanternlight outlining the curves of her impudent body ... the bold swell of her breasts, the shadowed delta of her cheeky loins ... molded tightly within the same striped calico wrapper as before, now without an apron. Her hair was freshly washed and combed, Ki noticed as he approached, and *whoof!* she had doused herself in some pleasing, if overpowering, fragrance. Which was fine by Ki, who reckoned he must smell funky-ripe after chousing strays all day.

She gestured and he followed her inside, upstairs to the second floor, into the rear corner bedroom. He looked about him, unseeing. The lumpy, white-painted ironpipe bed; the oval framed mirror above the washstand, its silvering gone in patches like moles; the battered carved-oak chest of drawers. He remembered the room from his search of the house, and didn't need the lamp Beth was lighting to remember the room as eminently forgettable.

61

"It isn't much," she allowed, "but it's yours from now on."

"Whoa," he said. "Back up a little. What is this?"

"It wasn't my idea, Ki. The hands thought it would be best."

"What would?"

"That you should stay over in the house instead of with them," she replied, opening the cabinet at the bottom of the washstand. "They think it's dangerous for me to be here alone."

"You mean the crew has assigned me here?"

"That's about it."

"Who do they think they are?" Ki stared out the window across the rear yard, at the moonlit waddies on their bench before the bunkhouse. And they stared back, contentedly. He yanked down the window-shade. "Well, I assign you to the bunkhouse instead."

"Don't be vulgar," Beth chided. She had taken a big, square blue bottle and two handleless cups from the cabinet, and now was pouring the cups full.

"They want to see you married; that's what it is, isn't it?"

Frostily, she said, "If it is, it's sure-certain not my idea."

"Hitched to anyone. Just so they had a man in the big house besides your uncle." Crinkles came into the corners of his eyes, and his lips quirked in a silent laugh at the sheer tomfoolery of it. "They're hoping it's dangerous for us to be alone together, and I get snared with my pants down. So to speak."

"That'll be enough of that, Ki." She looked distressed as she handed him a cup. "Although I really can't blame you for thinking improper of me," she added humbly, gravitating toward the bed with her cup and the bottle. "In Chicago, no decent lady ever visited with a man in his bedchamber."

"If there's one thing the frontier does, it strips away the unessentials. Here your word is your bond." Sitting down beside her, Ki took a sip from his cup. A trail of fired gunpowder seemed to flash into his throat, explode at the back of his nose, even explore his ears. He rasped, "What is it?"

"A little fever elixir I found when tidying up."

"Fever medicine?"

"Uncle Yokum's, but I recall Papa sometimes dosed himself with the same remedy," she explained, slipping off her shoes. "Papa swore it worked wonders when he'd been under a strain. When he fixed the smokepipe, or our cat had her litter in the walls."

Ki read the label on the bottle. MOTHER GAL- LAGHER'S MEDICAMENT, AGUE, JAUNDICE, SCROFULA, PALSY, PUERPERAL FEVER, ETC., 87% ALCOHOL. No wonder it worked wonders, he thought—eighty- seven percent.

"Papa would've thrown a two-bottle fit over our consortin'," Beth mused pensively. "So would Unk, I expect. Family always think the worst. That'd be the real shame, considering we're deeply indebted to you, we are."

"You don't owe me anything."

"I know better, Ki. I chatted with the hands while you were out riding." Beth swallowed a generous dollop of Mother Gallagher's, her eyes plaintively wide over the rim of the cup. "If Uncle Yokum's slickered out of his ranch," she fretted, "it's bound to break his heart, and that's bound to break my heart.

And there we'd be, friendless, castaways 'mongst the alien corn."

"Amongst the alien cows."

"You won't let them do that to us, will you? You'll be a friend." Her slim leg pressed against Ki's thigh as she leaned close, yearning. Her perfume was intoxicating, like an aromatic and heady wine, and her voice was vibrant with emotion. "From here on I'm going to need a friend. To hold on to. To give me strength. And in return, I . . . I'd do anything for a friend."

What a bodacious tease, Ki thought. The little minx nestled against his chest, her face uptilted, gazing at Ki with imploring eyes while giving him a restrained, mischievous smile. And there she hesitated, evidently wanting Ki to make the first move. So, sliding his hand over her shoulder, he kissed her gently, and she responded with a hungry enthusiasm, the pressure of her young body like an eager promise.

Their kiss was long, and Beth returned his with interest, harder, breath quickening, softly panting. Ki shifted his lips from her mouth to her throat, and began laving down her neck. "No, no . . ." she mewed, wriggling without drawing away. Then he moved to her breasts, which had preoccupied him so tantalizingly. "Mustn't . . . want to . . . can't help," she gasped. "Stop."

Ki stopped and sat up, chuckling. "Why, I thought you told me you'd do anything for a friend—friend."

Beth regarded him and then lowered her gaze—partly in assumed modesty, partly to see the state of his readiness, which perhaps alarmed her. "I did . . . but I thought you wouldn't hold me to it. It's not right you should make me, you know you shouldn't take advantage." Her eyes were crystal and blurred, and her delicate rosebud lips sagged laxly open. "I suppose I have no choice."

"You're talking nonsense," Ki said, smiling gravely. "It's give and take, remember? No one obligated to anyone."

With a low, throaty whimper, Beth crushed against him, frantically clenching in wild, unrestrained passion. Ki became aroused and yet was growing weary of her wanton, dizzy dalliancing. He wondered how far he could get with her, or rather, how far she'd go before turning off again. In any case, the quickest cure seemed to be a dose like before, so he enfolded her in a strong clasp and bent to kiss her.

Beth thrashed in his arms, mouth glued to his, eyes closed, nostrils quivering. She breathed in, moaning with pleasure, and her very eagerness fired Ki on. He extended his tongue tentatively, gingerly. She accepted, her lips parting, sending shivers of delight through him as his hot probe went deep into her mouth. Ki kept waiting for Beth to break their embrace, but she went on holding him, their mouths meshed tightly, until finally Ki rose for air.

"Please let this be enough, though . . . I can't resist you, please, let me be. . . ." she whispered, making big, wet sweeps of her lips across his mouth. "But no, I have to bare everything to you, don't I, Ki?"

"Why, Beth, you're suggesting things to order! You want to be forced to take off your clothes, don't you?"

"I have to take off my clothes, don't I? You're forcing me to bare everything right out here in the light. . . ." She was crooning to herself, her face suffused as she sat up and began unbelting, unbuckling, and undoing tiny eyehooks galore.

Ki dealt more quickly and quietly with his clothes, and was peeled to the raw in short order. He lay back, watching Beth finish her strip, thinking he must be a damn fool to be going along with her loco game. But what the hell, if Beth had to play Denial in order to loosen up, the only one she was kidding was herself. And a stiff prick knows no conscience, or sense of decency or danger, either.

"Everything!" Beth finally disentangled herself from her wrapper. Ki let his eyes feast on the gleaming alabaster of her body. She held her breasts in her hands, cupping their undersides and pushing the taut nipples out, then leaning over him and rubbing her breasts against his chest. "You wouldn't let me stop now, would you? I've got to *do* everything, I suppose."

Easing closer over him, Beth parted her lips and tasted his mouth again. This time she offered her tongue, moaning with the sheer heaven of it. She pushed him slowly back until he was lying flat. Then, moving down, she closed her mouth over his erection. Her hot, smooth, thrilling closure of sucking warmth forced Ki to squirm with growing passion. Beth put her hands under his hips and encouraged his movements, giving with his upward thrusts, taking as much as she could. She brought her tongue into play, touching his tip ever so lightly, then darting back as if too shy to continue. Then, clamping her mouth over him as tightly as she could without causing pain, Beth commenced a pumping action that drew little gasps out of him, and very near to a helluva lot more.

"You better quit while you're ahead," he panted.

She laughed, low, liquid. Lying full length on him, she pushed his hardness toward her warm, soft depths, clinging to him, reaching between them for his rigid shaft so she could guide it into her loins. In return, Ki lunged upward in sheer lust. She moaned in her eagerness and pushed her hips and thighs downward to take him, deep and hot and sliding, far up inside her pulsating belly.

Ki gripped her shoulders, his fingers digging in as Beth gasped with pleasure. Her firm, rounded buttocks rose from his loins in a smooth, sinuous arch, then pressed down, down, and drove his spearing manhood wetly into her. Her inner thighs and delta were greedy and slippery for more to fill her hungry cavern. The fulfilling length of Ki's erection was given up reluctantly, until all save the head was exposed for an instant, then it was reclaimed until her flaxen-hair was pressed tightly against his curls.

Beth moaned with every long, downward thrust of her hips. Ki was in the throes of imminent release, and his hands locked spasmodically around her tautly undulating buttocks, pulling her down with urgent power, grinding her tight, forcing every bit of himself into her, driving . . . driving. . . .

"Don't stop! Lordy, not yet!" Beth pleaded loudly. Ki felt her inner sheath contracting spasmodically from her erupting orgasm, the gripping pulsations milking him to climax. He spurted deep up inside her while she was sobbing and howling like a mountain banshee, pounding on his chest with her fists. And even after they were both good for nothing, Beth was still shrieking deliriously, "Don't stop!"

"Enough," Ki cautioned. "The crew will think I'm beating you."

Quieting to a sigh, Beth collapsed on top of him. He hugged her tight until she stopped shuddering and twitching. A while after that, she rolled off him and onto her back, snuggling close, damp with sweat, her fingers entwined with his.

"Ki?"

"Mm."

Shyly, she asked, "Was I good?"

"Very good."

"Honest? In Chicago—" she started.

"I know," Ki said. "Back in Chicago you do it differently."

Chapter 6

Early that same morning, while Ki was riding to the M-Over-Y, Jessie was taking her measure of the Anvil with Rawhide Avalon. She also was taking the first chance she could get to stash the incriminating canister of black powder that lay in her saddlebags. The opportunity came, but not quickly or easily, for during the short breaks when Rawhide wasn't keeping her company, there always seemed to be one or so of the crew around within eyeshot.

The crew paid her little or no attention, on the whole, though she wasn't about to risk being seen, even inadvertently. They griped and bantered among themselves, clad in worn range clothes, with utilitarian gunbelts and various second-hand pistols toted high, non-gunfighter style. Like the hands last night, they looked like what they were, Jessie was certain: damned good, honest laboring men. Trouble had made them harder and warier than normal, so she couldn't blame them for ignoring her, especially when they appeared none too sure of what to make of her presence, other than to resent it somewhat. Yet they were never rude or hostile, and welcomed her after a fashion—all except the foreman, Long Tom Hughes; and the ranch wrangler, called Cayuse Sumpter.

A stocky, turtle-jawed, messy-looking man, Sumpter was so bowlegged that a beer barrel could have fit between his knees. Horse chores occupied him around the stables and corrals, though it seemed to Jessie he kept crossing her path throughout the yard. Sumpter was at least tolerable as a horse handler, she judged; unfortunately, he was also at best tolerable, his horsemanship only fair to mid-dlin', nothing to crow about. He made an impact, however, with the glaring malice in his eyes and in his hostile demeanor, from first sight. Jessie guessed Sumpter hated women, maybe, or strangers, or both. But whatever his grudge, his virulent rancor was striking whenever they chanced to glimpse each other.

Jessie saw little of Long Tom Hughes, though she could feel his eye on her at intervals, in a baleful regard. She sensed the foreman to be honest, loyal, and implacably distrustful. What's more, he was fighter, belligerent by nature and with a temper that might be explosive if unchecked. It did not add to her sense of security when she saw Hughes in whispered talk with Cayuse, or later at noontime, when Hughes spoke to her as she was going in for lunch.

"Didn't take long to get acquainted," Hughes commented, managing to make it sound mighty insulting, the way he said it. "Rawhide's the salt of the earth, and if somebody hurt or took advantage of him, I'd feel need to go after that body and settle on my own, in my own style. 'Course, long as he vouches for you, Miz Starbuck, his say-so is plenty enough for me."

Jessie refrained from giving the foreman some say-so of her own, figuring what she had in mind wouldn't exactly soothe the situation between them.

She lunched with Rawhide on another one of Bertha's crippler meals. They and the dining table groaned under the onslaught of serving bowls and platters heaped so high as to be startling—savory chuck roast, boiled cabbage, fried potatoes with onions, buttered beets, buttered carrots, buttered biscuits the size of teacups, washed down with buttermilk by the pitcher and polished off with prune-and-rice pudding.

They were starting dessert when Bertha bustled in, all a-tizzy. "Visitors arrivin', sir! Dep'ty Voight and that Pierce bloke, with three bullies."

Rawhide sprang up. "I'll be right back, Jessie."

"We'll both be right back," she said, standing.

Jessie accompanied Rawhide out to the porch. Ahead in the yard she saw five men just dismounting from their horses. Gathering along the sidelines were Cayuse Sumpter and a couple of other Anvil hands who happened to be around the yard, and Long Tom Hughes, who had come striding in to stand at the foot of the porch steps, scowling at the five.

Carefully, dispassionately, Jessie sized up the arrivals. Deputy Voight was advancing to the fore, obviously to prevent trouble as the other four approached.

Another was an angular man, with a chiseled face already gone to dumplings of age at the corners of his jaw. Clad in tan canvas pants and a long, loose jacket of coffee brown corduroy, this was undoubtedly Felix Pierce, looking the image of a prosperous stockman. Almost. Somehow Pierce was a shade immaculate for a working stockman, who would've had baggy pockets in that jacket, filled with just about everything, and at least one stain on his pants. Pierce also looked the sort not given to hear any such criticism. His tightly pursed lips and his hard ferret eyes, sunken behind a rosy blade of a nose, bespoke a man who could never be wrong. The world could be wrong, but he couldn't.

The three other men joined Pierce, spread and a little to one side. The scar-faced 'breed that Ki had dumped in mud was there, cleaned up but none the handsomer. The other two were a pair of heavy-set, hunch-shouldered strangers to Jessie: one had cheeks covered with thin dirty hair, and blinked through bloodshot eyes; his partner was a gaunt-jawed, loose-lipped man who chewed rhythmically on nothing. Two of the trio wore denims, vests, and soiled cotton shirts, while the chewer had on scuffed chaps and a whipcord blouse. Their guns were tied low. The chewer was a two-gun man.

Rawhide was frowning at the deputy. "If you care to traffic with evil companions, Voight, that's your concern. But I'd be just as happy if you didn't drag none of this riffraff into my sanctum."

The bloodshot man took instant offense. "Who you callin' riffraff?" he flared indignantly. "I've a mind to dust you around, mosshorn."

"No vi'lence," Voight ordered forcefully.

72

"Same goes for y'all as for Kuttner," Pierce added, regarding his men. "We got to show ourselves friendly, if we're to try settling our wrangle."

Right then and there Jessie sensed trouble ahead. Pierce was sounding too noble by half, reminding her of those tentshow reformers who managed to get pie out of piety. He was blowing smoke to bury the real reason he came here, whatever that was, but why else hide motives if not to conceal trouble?

The Block-P boys openly promised trouble. Siding Pierce, the 'breed sneered wolfishly, scar livid on his lobo face, though he retained enough of the cowhand to appear almost human. Crueler, more depraved, Kuttner and the two-gunner smirked nastily at Rawhide, munching him with their predatory eyes. Jessie knew them for what they were—bullies, just as Bertha had tagged them; gun-thugs who fought only in pairs, against those they considered weaker prey. Rawhide and his few unskilled hands, they thought, would make easy fodder to bait into gunplay, before witnesses and the law.

Or so Jessie perceived, of a sudden. Her impressions proved out as Pierce wound up his sermonizing with: "We come just to talk to Mr. Avalon, just to Mr. Avalon," he declared. "Who's that with him?" He gestured toward Jessie.

"Maybe she's the old honcho's betrothed," the two-gunner remarked. "Maybe she rules the roost here, and's the one you want to powwow with."

"Maybe I'm just a wayfaring stranger passing through," Jessie countered. "But it won't cost me anything to listen."

"I listened enough," Voight snapped. "Muzzle your smart-mouthed boys, Pierce; nobody asked

73

Block-P's opinion. Nobody invited you to come."
When Rawhide started to speak, he warned, "Don't
you mess with me, neither. I'm the law, and the law's
had a bellyful of you two at each other's throats."

"We ain't at his throat, he's at our'n," Rawhide
charged.

"It so happens, Rawhide," the deputy said, his
voice chilling, "there're two sides to every question.
I don't have no real proof that Block-P has been up
to nothing, like you claim. On t'other hand, I got
grounds to believe Anvil raided Block-P last night,
exploding a bunch of cattle and two of their night-
crew to smithereens."

The Anvil hands erupted in furor for a moment.
Jessie kept still and wondered: Had men really died
last night? The riderless horses and shredded apparel
made it seem plausible, even credible, when she in-
cluded the black powder cannister she'd cached. She
noticed, then, Long Tom Hughes ahead, and Sumpter
over with the hands, both glancing venomously at
her, while the uproar quietened and Rawhide retorted, "For the last time, Anvil ain't in the blasting
business!"

"It's got renegade hands, then," Voight con-
tended. "Since sunup I been out wading in that
bloody carnage amidst hunks of cow carcass, strips
of clothing, and what pieces remain of Ed Pucheim
and Jinglebob Ashburton."

"Them two?" Rawhide said, with a derisive snort.
"From what I knowed of 'em, I'd hazard Pucheim
and Ashburton each suspicioned there was a reward
on the other, and blew themselves to bits trying to
capture one 'nother."

Pierce gave a bellow. "They were fine, decent

hands and ever'body thought swell of 'em at the Block-P. Besides, by a great stroke of luck, Wahoo Delgardo spied an Anvil man leaving the scene."

"Who?" Jessie asked.

"Not yet sure," Voight admitted. "He was too far to snap-identify."

"Then how did Delgardo know he was an Anvil man? Was he wearing an Anvil uniform?"

"I don't think murder is funny," Voight objected. "Not at all."

"Murder?" Jessie queried. "You said you found strips of clothing, but how do you know they belong to Pucheim and Ashburton? Did you find their boots or hats, or how about their guns?"

"Well, not exactly, but—"

"Did you find heads or feet or hands?" Jessie pressed, questions and answers emerging from haunting memories of the site last night. "Did you find anything you can swear is even human, or any other grounds to suspect Anvil?"

Voight opened his mouth as if to snap at a fly, then closed it again and said through his teeth, "Nope. I may never. But I'll do my best to find what's what."

Jessie smiled. Most lawmen would've guffed, "I'm on a crucial lead, with proof pending," or at least looked inscrutably satisfied, but Deputy Voight looked miserable. He might or might not be incompetent, but Jessie was certain he was honest and conscientious, not a gutless tool of the rich and powerful.

"Don't worry," Pierce assured Voight, "Wahoo swears he knows the hombre, and it'll come back to him any time. Still, it sure goes to show you the crews at both ranches are fomenting agin' each other. We could work up to something mighty bad for the whole range." He turned to Rawhide. "Don't you agree?"

"We'll cross that bridge when we come to it," Rawhide answered.

"When it's already afire?" Pierce shook his head. "You can't cross a burning bridge. It's too late then."

"Is that why you came to talk? To threaten me?"

"I came to ask you to cooperate."

"Me'n you?" Rawhide looked vaguely nauseated. "Whatever for?"

"For sake of peace and tranquility. In the spirit of goodwill, here's my final offer to the Anvil. We'll let your foreman, Hughes, and my man at the Block-P, talk it over and set the right price. Nobody can say that wouldn't be plenty fair, and it'd put a halt to more unnecessary ruckus and row."

Rawhide was in such a boil now that he gagged. Finally he rasped, "Fat chance, me giving over my spread and apologize, just to pacify you."

"That's the way you put it," Kuttner scoffed. "Mr. Pierce puts it different. What's your lady-love's notion?"

They had come for blood and trouble, nothing else.

Jessie didn't want any wild shooting, didn't want Rawhide dying in her lap. She stepped down off the porch, saying, "Oh, I'm not his lady-friend. I'm just here because I haven't anywhere else to go. Sounds like a splendid idea. Under one ownership, there wouldn't be any strife atwixt you."

A growl came up from the knot of Anvil hands.

Long Tom Hughes railed, "What kind of viper are you?" as she went by, on into the yard.

"You blackguardin' her?" the two-gunner rapped out, provocatively sauntering toward Jessie. Long Tom Hughes seemed of two minds, and wavered a second. Pierce spoke up that second, pretending the call-out never happened.

"Exactly my point, ma'am. You hit what I was getting at," he told Jessie loftily. "Gun-strife can be a dose of miseries. I know. I've seen it."

"I'm sure you have."

"Mm. An' so far I've been able to hold my crew in check. But it could be this latest is the last straw. That this is the spark that sets it off."

"Set the straw off, you mean?"

Pierce ignored her reply. "Unfortunately, Mr. Avalon ain't sensible an' agreeable to my buying Anvil."

"That's only one angle. Your idea has another just as good."

"What?"

"Mr. Avalon buys Block-P from you."

Pierce went iron stiff. "Very droll."

"It's a pip," Kuttner hooted. "Expandin' the puny Anvil by adding the Block-P is like expandin' a useless ol' moose tail by adding a moose."

The two-gunner was ambling up to Jessie now, grinning snidely. "You got rich fancies, gal. The Block-P costs more'n lace an' ribbons an' lilac parfoom soap."

He acted at ease, but Jessie bet the blood ran hot in him. She bet her life on it, and on her training with Ki. Smiling equably, she came to stop about

77

five feet in front of the man and asked pleasantly, "What's your name?"

"I ain't got no name," he said, winking at Kuttner.

"Your family couldn't make up its mind, I imagine," Jessie said sociably. "I had a dog like that once. I kept putting it off, and putting it off. And ended up by calling him Spunky."

Something seemed to snap inside him, like a loosened hair-trigger. Bang, thataway. He stepped back impulsively, instinctively drawing right-handed with the speed of a striking rattler, his left poised to grab his reserves.

Alert for action, Kuttner shouted immediately, "Keep your stink-fingers away from your iron, feller!" He was yelling at the porch, trying to cover his partner's cross-draw and his own stabbing pull with his mock-angry alarm.

That was their style, okay. Take no chances, give no breaks, and you live the longest. Neither Rawhide nor Long Tom Hughes had made any move whatever.

Time telescoped, and seemed later never to have existed. In a lunge, drawing with frantic speed as she moved, Jessie clenched the two-gunner's gunwrist with her free hand and swung it outward, at the same time stepping full into him, spreading the armpit further with the wedge of his shoulder. It was in this position, with her pistol flat against the two-gunner's side, that she shot Kuttner, who was standing a little behind.

It was Kuttner who at that instant had had the drop on everyone else, his trigger-finger squeezing, his revolver targeting Rawhide and Long Tom Hughes, his mind no doubt calculating how to pick off the survivor. They were fumbling for their weapons, and the

Anvil hands were slower still, but not even Deputy Voight's swift draw could catch up in time. Pierce and the 'breed were no slouches, either, Pierce drawing a Merwin & Hulbert .38 from under his long coat, and the 'breed unlimbering a .44-40 Remington. They'd have had them out and leveled in another second or two. So Jessie had made Kuttner her primary target, and had nailed him first.

The two-gunner tussling with her now Jessie shot next, up under the ribcage, ramming her gun muzzle into the man's clothes as she fired. He was dead before he hit the ground.

Livid with vehemence and disbelief, Pierce and the 'breed brought their revolvers to bear on Jessie. The Anvil men were gripping their pistols, covering Pierce and the 'breed in a dead certain crossfire from the porch and sidelines. Jessie, her gunhammer at full cock, centered on Pierce.

"Hold it!" Voight demanded sternly. "Shooting's over!"

The savagery and hatred in the air was almost unbearably tight, and Jessie felt it was touch and go. For an instant she wasn't sure whether they were going to obey the deputy or not. In a split second, she could be on the ground, too, mouth open in a gout of blood, attracting flies.

The 'breed was panting, his eyes bulging like hardboiled eggs.

Pierce kept his wits, though his face was darkened in stiff, clotted rage. "Stow it," he ordered the 'breed, and put his .38 away, proclaiming, "The day of judgment is coming, and soon. Then she'll get hers, along with the others."

Grudgingly the 'breed obeyed. All of them—the

cowhands, Long Tom Hughes—holstered their weapons. All except Deputy Voight, who kept a casual hold on his revolver, appearing lax but sure as hell ready, as he glanced over at Jessie, asking, "You okay?"

She nodded shakily. "I'll ride to town, if that's what you mean."

"Yep, got to follow it up. Looks like justifiable self-protection," Voight said dryly. "You got yourself a witness or two."

"She sure has," Rawhide said. "Bring on your courts and prosecutors and stacks o' bibles. Miz Starbuck escaped only by the grace o' God, never given no warning when that sidewinder started his draw first."

"She scared him," the 'breed said. "I'd have drawed first, too."

"And you'd have had just about as much luck," Pierce responded bitterly. "This lady ain't no lady, she's a sharpshootin' gunwoman."

Jessie looked shocked. "Oh, I hardly think so," she demurred, shaking her head. "I don't care for loud noises."

"Then how'd you manage to kill 'em?" Pierce demanded. "Both of 'em, one, two, like swatting flies!"

"No, swatting is different. It happened all so fast, but I'm sure I know how I did it," Jessie confided. "I removed my firearm from its purse—this leather thing here, y'see—and jiggled this little thing down here that's like a curved nail. That's the trigger. That makes it go off."

The listeners there looked paralyzed, the lot of them.

"That's enough of that," Voight said, after a lapse. "Pierce, you two take the bodies and tie 'em on their horses. I'll bring 'em to Doc Lozier, and you can deal with 'em at the undertaker's tomorrow."

When that was done, Pierce and the 'breed mounted up. Pierce shifted in his saddle as he warned Rawhide, "Remember, you brought this on yourself, when you brought this hellcat to kill Block-P men."

Then as Pierce turned to go, Jessie said to Rawhide, "You think he came as a peacemaker?"

Rawhide didn't answer.

Still ignoring Pierce, Jessie said, "He came to make the trouble deeper. He only pretended to bargain to make it look decent afterward. You can't head him off, no matter what you do."

Pierce and the 'breed left at a gallop, without saying goodbye.

When they were gone, Deputy Voight said to Jessie, "Whilst we're on the subject, before we start back, are you actually some sort of Deadeye Dolly?"

"No," she replied seriously, not offended. "Not in the least."

"Well, you outdrew the Pend Orielle Kid."

"Oh, the two-gun man, was that his name? Who was he?"

"A professional who used to hang around Grant's Pass. I always heard he was a little better than tol'rable good."

"Gracious, and me scared out of my wits, all a-tremble," Jessie said with wide, round eyes. "The wonders of accident can be hard to believe."

"Specially with you, who probably never pulled a gun in her life."

"Never," Jessie said. She added, "That I can recall."

"Well, anyway, in any event," Voight said with a worried sigh, "the day of judgment Pierce spoke of. It's come."

Chapter 7

The sun was long down, and it was moon-washed night when Jessie arrived back at Suicide Spread.

She rode into the cluster of yellow windows that were the Anvil ranch buildings, drawing up by the stable and looking about her. There was a barn lantern on an upended barrel near the open stable doors, but there was no one in sight, no one moving within the stable or ranchyard.

Leading her horse inside, Jessie gave it a rubdown, feed, and a stall. On her way out, she was going by the barn lantern when something sang past her shoulder. The loops of a riata settled over her head, snagging her tight and jerking her off her feet.

Before Jessie could react, Anvil crewmen swarmed in, tackling her, dragging her off to one side, away from the lantern-lit doorway. It was futile to struggle with her arms lassoed tight to her sides, though she got in a few good kicks that raised painful grunts. Opening her mouth to scream, she heard the guttural voice of Cayuse Sumpter rasp out, "Jeez, don't let her scream!" One of the other men rashly clamped a callused hand over her face, and Jessie bit his palm.

The man screamed, letting go.

Jessie was shoved up against a vegetable crib, Sumpter holding her roped while the ranch hands crowded close. Refusing to be intimidated, she resisted strenuously, to no avail but to the annoyance of her captors.

"Quit it," one of them barked. "Behave, and we'll slack off."

"You don't," another warned, "and we'll hog-tie you to the crib and stuff your mouth shut with all our sweaty 'kerchiefs."

Jessie subsided, her baffled eyes burning into them.

As the men glared wolfishly, Sumpter cast loose his rope. "I'll keep it handy in case she forgets and tries something. Hope she does."

"Let her. She can't pull no female wiles that'll trance us to forget," a waddie growled, "'cept maybe forget she's a female."

"Now, listen, gunma'arm, we're aiming to have us a look-see."

"Yeah, empty your pockets if you don't want us poking through 'em."

In a black rage, Jessie turned out her pockets. Her saddlebags, other gear, and the horse stall were searched, but the men didn't seem to find what they were hunting for, and gathered around her again, hard-eyed, grim-lipped.

Sumpter leaned close, the whites of his eyes showing like the eyes of an animal. "C'mon, you," he snarled. "What'd you do with that canister of blasting powder? We know you got it."

Jessie's eyes narrowed to a leaping spark, and she was about to demand they tell her how they knew, when there came a commotion from the back. More men thrust into the circle—the rest of the now awakened crew, including Long Tom Hughes and Rawhide Avalon, who scowled darkly as he regarded Sumpter and those with him.

"What in thunderous hell is the meaning of this, boys?" he yelled.

For a moment there was no answer; then Jessie spoke: "I'd like to know too, Rawhide. We've got some sorry misunderstandings that need clearing up."

"Sorry! They'll get down on their marrowbones, groveling regrets and apologies, for this stunt," Rawhide replied, hard and incisive. "What I want to hear is who set this off and why! Start clacking, or I'll fire y'all!"

For a breathing instant the crewmen with Cayuse Sumpter remained silent. Then one of them grumbled and replied, "Well, boss, I hate to break the news, but this woman, she's really Felix Pierce's wench, sent here to spy on us."

"Are you loco? She plugged two of his Block-P gunmen!"

"Sure, all that was only a blind."

"Come clean, Norris, you ain't going to bamboozle your way out of this."

"It's gospel, boss," Norris insisted. "It's like Cayuse was telling us: her shootout gives Pierce his

85

excuse to ride riot over Anvil. She had us all fooled, but Cayuse bet we could catch her dead to rights, with a can of black powder that she'd saved from her blasting cows last night."

"I see," Rawhide said. "Well, let's see the proof you found."

Norris murmured something inaudible. The others made no comment, and Sumpter seemed suddenly stricken deaf, concentrating on rolling a cigarette.

Rawhide grew an angry red. "I see you roughed her, I see you tied her up, but I don't see no canister o' powder."

Another embarrassed puncher admitted, "No, there wasn't anything on her or in her belongings, boss. Cayuse, though, he bet she was going to plant the can, as evidence we did to Pierce's cattle, and maybe that's what she's done already somewheres."

Rawhide gave a derisive snort. "Did any of you boneheads ever stop to wonder how Cayuse knows about a canister and things?" He riveted Sumpter with his eyes. "You couldn't have known, not unless you knew there was a canister unaccounted for. Or unelss you were there, and saw Miz Jessie. Which is it?"

Sumpter gazed at the crew as though Rawhide was making a gross blunder.

"Answer the boss," Hughes ordered. "How'd you know so all-fired much?"

"You got it mixed up," Sumpter finally managed with a false heartiness. "I'm Anvil, I'm with you guys. She's the outsider trying to sneak in."

"Nothing to do with her," Rawhide said. "This's 'tween me and you."

Sumpter grew pugnacious. "You got nothing agin'

me. Nothing." His eyes were roving now, to Rawhide, to Jessie, to Long Tom Hughes and the flanking crewmen. *He's cornered now and he knows it,* Jessie thought; *his only concern is survival.* He said, "Maybe I'd best walk away till tempers cool. I won't bear no grudge if you don't."

"That's nice," Rawhide said, stepping forward.

"What're you aiming to do?"

"To listen to you telling us all you know, Cayuse."

Norris added bitterly, "We'll keep the rope handy, in case you forget."

Sumpter was smoking the last of his cigarette. Rawhide was reaching to disarm him when Sumpter took the cigarette stub from his mouth and dropped it casually on the ground. In the same careless motion, he put out his foot and stepped on it. It was a common, natural action—except that he used his left hand. His right hand swung for his belly-holstered revolver, his eyeballs seeming to protrude and his mouth contorting spasmodically. As he drew, he shifted to grab Rawhide as a hostage and a shield between himself and the others.

Alert for just such trickery, Jessie caught his left-handed switcheroo and saw that from her angle she couldn't fire at Sumpter without risking Rawhide. Instead she was on him in a diving lunge, right hand twisting Sumpter's gun wrist, left arm clenching his waist. They rocked back and forth in a sort of death embrace, Jessie trying to force the weapon around and back, Sumpter, gristle-muscled, fighting to bring it to the fore. It was in this swaying, the gun momentarily behind Sumpter, when the trigger fell, a cartridge exploded with a roar, and a big slug plowed up through the back of Sumpter's skull, smashing it.

Cayuse Sumpter fell, wilting terribly, and mounded himself grotesquely on the ground.

To the stupefied Anvil crewmen, Jessie said, "Why didn't you rush in to disarm him?"

They stood silently. Some chagrined, some gawking, a few muttering but saying nothing. Rawhide was right spritely as he recoiled from the body, then turned to Jessie with a vast grin of relief.

"I'm beholden, Miz Jessie, you salvaged my hide. Hate to admit it, but truth is that Sumpter had been worrying me a trifle lately."

"Worrying you how?"

"He'd been flashing more money than I paid him."

"Did you think he was being double-paid?"

"No, I figured he was gambling. Now it's clear he took my wages and a neighboring rancher's, too," Rawhide said cryptically. Frowning at his crew, he ordered: "Muck up here and haul Sumpter back to the toolshed, and tomorrow we'll take care of him—and damn good riddance. I hope you galoots are feelin' sorrily ashamed of yourselves. You got cause to be."

Yet Jessie wondered, when she retired to the guest bedroom a short while later, what Rawhide Avalon would have said if he had known that Sumpter had told the truth—that she had the cannister, and had hidden it just beyond the yard, though not as evidence against the Anvil. Sumpter must have seen her pick it up. Well, that was that. . . .

The guest bedroom was at one end of the main house. It had a big brass bed with bolsters and a tasseled coverlet, and its windows were open to the yard and wide to the full moon, silvery and luminous. On the marble top of the washstand was a bouquet of velvet pansies in a cut-glass tumbler, which Jessie moved aside to pour a half-basin of water and take a quick cat-bath. Removing her boots and holstered shellbelt, she loosened her jeans, doused the lamp, and climbed into bed.

And lay there, unable to sleep. Her mind was too distressed by the grim events, too disturbed by Pierce's ways and means, to let her relax. Long after she should have dozed off, Jessie was wondering if Sumpter had left behind any hint of a clue, any trace of evidence that might catch Pierce short. Probably not, but possibly it was worth a try. Messing it up, though, was the chance that Pierce had other spies planted on Anvil. To get around that, she had to go prowling now, without anyone the wiser, snooping about before anyone could cover up.

Climbing out of bed, Jessie dressed and eased along the hall to the side door by the kitchen, padding carefully, boots in hand so as not to disturb Rawhide. With equal thoughtfulness, she glided outside and across to the two-holer shanty that served the main house. It was small but high-powered. At its half-moon door, she took a whiff and promptly lost all inclination for her nocturnal call of nature. Besides, the yard appeared empty, the ranch slumbering quietly under the big, white harvest moon.

So peaceful a view was it that Jessie decided to take the longer, scenic route on her return to the house. Keeping to the shadows as much as possible, she headed back in a roundabout detour via the corrals and barn where Sumpter had often worked. Abruptly she flattened against the wall of the barn, making herself small. A figure drifted by her. In the midnight moonglow, she could see the range-clad form of a medium-big man, though his face was shaded and indistinct under the broad brim of his flat-crowned hat.

Jessie followed him cautiously, stealthily. He had not come from the bunkhouse or the main house; so whoever this bravo was, he was not Anvil and he was no doubt coming to make trouble. She could have drilled him then and there, but he might have partners hidden nearby; it would be better to go slow, to learn what she could of the man and his motive before he grew aware of her.

Stalking, Jessie saw the man halt and lie down prone in the cover of a sumac bush about five feet from the main house. Just above was the window of Rawhide's bedroom. Jessie sucked in her breath, pistol in hand. The man rose abruptly and moved forward to stoop by the foundation, doing something she could not quite make out, although she had managed to work up within a few feet of the man.

There came a spark, and a match flared alight. She caught a brief glimpse of the man's face, slightly more than medium-ugly, squint-eyed, bulbous-jawed, his lips peeled back from his teeth in a soundless snarl.

Then something hissed and sputtered. Blasting powder! The man was lighting the long fuse that strung from a powder canister.

At that moment Jessie launched herself upward and out. She landed on the man's back like a tigress, and there came a startled curse as, cracking down on him with her gunbutt, Jessie felt the man go limp.

The fuse was sputtering merrily. Frantic, Jessie ground it out beneath her heel.

For that instant, in her anxiety to snuff the sparking danger, she was intent solely upon the fuse. Stunned but not out, the man took advantage of her preoccupation by scrambling to his feet and staggering at a run from the yard. Jessie glimpsed him fleeing, and, as she wheeled, drawing her pistol, gunflame lanced from the dimness and a slug droned past her ear.

Jessie shot the man just as he was on verge of getting away to do more meanness later. She shot him once by gunsight, and then, because the moon was suddenly dimmed by a wispy cloud veil, once more in the chest for surety. The man ran dead a half-step, then collapsed flat.

As if in a nightmare, Jessie saw another figure charging down from the porch, gun held high. She shouted, not wishing to be shot, mistaken for an enemy. It was Rawhide who answered her with a yell: "Hell's bells, what's doin'? That you, Miz Jessie?"

She yelled in answer, as there came a rumble of hoofs. Out of the bordering trees and undergrowth, men were lurching into their saddles by twos and threes. From the bunkhouse erupted the Anvil hands, gripping weapons, clamoring, startled and querulous as they tore after the mounting raiders.

"Some dozen of 'em, I calc'late," Rawhide yelled at Jessie.

Men cursed. The crack and rattle of gunfire beat upwards against the night sky. The Anvil crew had no time to go saddle up mounts, so they came charging afoot across the yard, while the raiders were trying frenziedly to regain control of their horses and vamoose. The raiders crashed through the underbrush, each man for himself, with the Anvil crew in hot-lead pursuit. Blistering salvoes of gunfire raged from the wooded area.

The staccato volleys tapered to the slam-slam of scattering shots. Then, by twos and threes, the Anvil crew came straggling back.

"We winged 'em aplenty," Jessie heard from nearby, and, turning, she saw that Long Tom Hughes was addressing her while he was heading for the man she'd hit. She started toward the body, too, meeting Hughes just about there.

"They've sure hit the high spots, skedaddling. They didn't loaf," Hughes told her. "Looks like you got the only kill." He rolled the body over with his foot. "Yep, another noble, big-hearted Block-P bastard. Max Sunderland."

Jessie regarded the medium-big, slightly-more-than-medium-ugly man. In death, his bulbous-jawed face looked relaxed, contented.

"This is what Sunderland's been working for all his life," Hughes said, hunkering as he checked the man's pockets. "And now he's got it." Hughes brought out a canister of black powder. "Well, look what else he's got. Now we know the dirty, hard work Pierce had sent him to do."

Just then Rawhide called out for Hughes. Answering, Hughes headed over to where Rawhide stood by the bedroom window, holding the canister with the burnt fuse. Jessie, left alone, gave a startled gasp a few moments later, when she came up with yet another canister. Turning it over to Rawhide and

Hughes, she kept a watchful eye on their faces as the two men examined the cans.

"Wal, shiver my vittles," Rawhide exclaimed. "They must've planned to blow me up in my bed, then blow up the bunkhouse and charge in a-gunning." He looked thoughtful. "We had some powder stolen, sure . . . but not this type."

The canister Sunderland had planted at the main house was identical to the one Hughes had found on him. Both were duplicates of the can Jessie had discovered by lucky happenstance—or so the men thought, and Jessie let them believe. She didn't need much luck, though, to remember her hiding place for the canister she'd found that first night. It only added up one way, that Felix Pierce had procured a covert supply of black powder somewhere.

The Anvil crewmen were gathering around, milling agitatedly as Rawhide filled them in, exhibiting the canisters and asserting, "Pierce must've blown up his own cattle! If Ed Pucheim and Jinglebob Ashburton were blasted, their own bunkmates did it. But I agree with Miz Jessie's suspicions, that they weren't killed a'tall, just their horses turned loose and so forth to make it seem like they'd bursted to kingdom come."

"That cussed Pierce almost got us jugged over it," Hughes added. "He schemed it that way to get Deputy Voight's backing, as well as the support of the law-abidin' folks hereabouts. He sure's been going to a lot of trouble."

"Yeah, and now tonight. If Pierce thinks this'll frighten me into selling, he's got another think coming. I'm in a fury."

"Like you're supposed to be," Jessie said, "if not dead or scared."

Hughes said, "I don't understand."

"I do," Rawhide said. "If nothing else, we'd be goaded into warpathin' around like lunatics, and they'd execute us in what would look like self-defense." He turned to Jessie. "Okay, you tell me what you want us to do."

"Take no risks. You're proud men, and proud men make green graves."

Bitterly Hughes said, "That's a shameful hard order to follow."

"You mean even no self-defense?" Rawhide asked wretchedly.

"Self-defense is a different matter," Jessie replied. "I mean just don't let them trick you into suicide. We'll teach them that trouble is receiving as well as giving. Their first lesson may come legally, from Deputy Voight."

Rubbing his jaw, Rawhide glanced over at the body. "You got a point, Miz Jessie. We'll go to town tomorrow and open that lawdog's eyes."

Chapter 8

Gray dawn went into silver dawn, and the silver had burned off in the sky to a medium-deep watery blue, clear and cloudless, when Jessie rode out of the ranchyard with Long Tom Hughes.

The bodies of Cayuse Sumpter and the Block-P man, Sunderlund, had already left by wagon for Unity. But Jessie wasn't heading there, not this time. No one was going to town besides a wagon driver and his helper, although the whole crew was hot to trot. For that reason among others, Jessie and Rawhide had decided it'd be better to stay put and have the deputy come out to them. So Hughes had assigned the hands their tasks for the day, then invited Jessie to accompany him on a ride.

"We'll take a tour of the east line," Hughes had told her. "We swing through that section regularly, on account of it borders the Block-P."

Jessie had accepted gladly, though she felt that Hughes didn't entirely mean it; that he asked her politely, pleasantly, but just out of courtesy.

Riding out, Hughes led Jessie on a circuit of the east boundary, wending north to south along a rough, twisty, single-file path. They wound through brush and timber; across gulches and hollows; over corrugated slopes where sage claimed the thin, rocky soil on the high banks, and grass grew lush in pocket meadows where runoff deposited richer soil. And as they loped on, Jessie still sensed an undercurrent of reserve, of reticence, running in the foreman. Maybe it was her imagination; anyway, she ignored it, staying companionable and showing interest in him.

Jessie was indeed interested with respect to his views as foreman. And the fact that he couldn't fully hide his feelings confirmed her initial impression of him as an open-faced, forthright man loyal to his ranch. Hughes stood tall; he didn't slink. He was smart, not shrewd. Perversely, by keeping his distance, he attracted her, challenging her to win his approval, arousing a closer awareness of him that edged on sexual appeal. Not that she had such intentions in mind, she thought hastily; and by his attitude, she doubted Long Tom was harboring any sort of amorous notions.

Gradually, though, Hughes seemed to grow friendlier and more talkative, explaining pungently how Rawhide was financially strapped. The Anvil range afforded evidence of his words. Livestock was scarce, for Rawhide had cut his herd dearly and sold cheaply in order to meet wages and expenses. His remaining cows were far from soup culls, but they weren't prime, juicy beeves, either, looking thin and scrawny after frequent stampedings by nightriders. If the cattle weren't hazed, they were swiped no matter how underweight, which indicated that the rustlers were out to ruin Anvil, not simply lift some stock for quick profit.

Presently the trail threaded a series of rimrock slopes, overlooking that wooded basin where the blasting had occurred. Hughes cautioned, "Best go slow and look sharp for Block-P'ers up through here. This's as near the hub of that buzzard nest as the Anvil line gets."

"Was it Pierce who built the Block-P?"

"Nope, his pappy. Rufus Pierce started his herd here many years ago, by cheating sad-sack immigrants out of their footsore cows. Rufus was the type of old-timer that all the other old-timers try to pretend never existed, and ever since his death a while back, his son has carried on the tradition. Felix Pierce is more the warlord than his pappy was. He likes to boss people, ride roughshod over 'em, making it look good with smarm and shine and money. And muscle. I don't know where he gets those so-called cowhands."

"I know where he gets them," Jessie said. "They come to him. Because they're the same type of animal."

They rode on silently across tableland that rippled with grass, juniper, and clearwater. In the distance smoky ridges rose hazy in the sun. It was a beautiful autumn morning. Shortly, Hughes pointed to a yonder crest that seemed to have two rock chimneys looming high, connected by an arch of stone.

"O'er there is Pierce's place. He sure owns the territory. I don't know what he'd do with Rawhide's land; it ain't that much and it ain't that good."

"But he wants the Anvil."

"He sure do."

"Then why?"

"Plain ol' power. Getting the Anvil proves he's stronger, and when he's got it, it makes him bigger," Hughes suggested, then shook his head. "Naw, it has to mean money to them somehow, or they wouldn't be trying to gun it through."

"They?"

"Yeah, Pierce and his banker pappy-in-law, Ingersoll. I'd hazard that Pierce figures to drive Rawhide to either sell out to him, or go borrow money from the bank. Ingersoll will loan it, but at twenty percent interest; then he'll refuse to renew the note if Rawhide can't pay when it falls due. They've pulled that bamboozle before, and they must expect it to pay off again this time. I wish I knew how come."

Soon after, they sighted a group of steers at some distance ahead. Hughes spurred toward them and yelled, motioning for Jessie to follow, but there were also some other cows bunched yonder in a draw. Jessie called that she'd go flush out this second group, and before the foreman could refuse her help, she veered off in their direction.

The distance was greater than it had seemed in the clear, winey air, and it took Jessie upwards of an hour before she was able to chouse the cattle free. By now the indian summer sun was at its zenith, glinting in a reflective shimmer off the pebbled rock of the long draw, and confusing her for a moment when she glimpsed a flick of movement at the far bend of the draw. Curious, wondering if maybe she'd overlooked a cow down there, Jessie rode to see what she could see. As she neared the corner, a ruffed grouse hen rose, clucking, and ran across in front of her. Jessie grinned to herself—

And riders barged round the blind curve at a floundering canter.

There were three of them, and they were almost onto her. They reined up like maniacs, so close that at first they seemed all enormous horses' chests and heads and bridles, bridle straps and brass buckles, flying streamers of slaver. Then the men loomed behind the horses' ears, dressed like cowhands. Their clothes and saddles had seen a lot of wear and riding. One, spiderlike, was all big chest and little bowlegs. One had the intense, burnished eyes of a lynx. The third, apparently the leader, was squat and muscular, his bloated-lipped mouth open in a scornful shout. All were carrying Henry lever action carbines, not in their rifle boots, but out and slantwise across the inside of their saddleforks, hair triggers ready for a snap shot.

"Looky here," the leader was shouting. "The gunbitch!" The carbine in his hand swung level, aiming at Jessie. "Shit, the Pend Oreille Kid always was a sucker for floozies."

There was no space to veer aside, and no time to, anyway. At so slight a distance it would be impossible for them to miss, Jessie knew, and this gunman had all but admitted they were here to shoot her on sight. She was going down, but she'd try to take at least one with her.

Her fingers went for her gunbutt as she kicked free of her saddle.

With a gloating sneer, the gunman squeezed the trigger.

The crack of a big-bore gunshot thundered in the narrow way.

Landing, rolling, Jessie came up firing instantly, instinctively, before being consicous of any wound or whether this was her last breath. She missed, but the gunman was no longer seated quite as he had been in the saddle. He was slumping in a lax fall, with half the crown of his head missing.

The spiderlike man was starting to bring his carbine to bear. Jessie shifted slightly and shot him, her slug ripping his throat to shreds as if from an inner explosion. The man's mount went into a small shy, cramming into his partner's mount. This one, the man with the burnished eyes, had his carbine butt almost to his armpit to draw his bead when Jessie blasted him. She shot him twice. Hip-shooting riflemen didn't worry Jessie too much; but bead-drawing riflemen did, sure as hell.

Jessie rose from her crouch, shaken and bewildered. By some inexplicable miracle, she had come through untouched. And the trio had wound up dead, the first stretched face-up under his horse's belly, the spiderlike one curled fetally on the ground, and the last man twisted, sprawling, entangled in his stirrup. Jessie untangled him.

Before she got any more surprises, Jessie reloaded her still-smoking pistol. She then inspected their horses, finding to no surprise that they bore the Block-P brand. She was removing the horses' bridles and bits when she heard a rider approaching. She aimed her pistol, preparing to fire.

"Don't shoot!" Long Tom Hughes yelled, heaving into view. He reined his cowpony to a stiff-legged halt. "That was positively a close one," he said breathlessly. "I had to make a helluva long shot to pop that feller, and thank Gawd I brung my 'Big Fifty' Sharps along instead of the usual saddle carbine."

"You?" Jessie said, eyeing Hughes closely. She holstered her pistol and daubed her shirt sleeve across her forehead. "Thanks."

"I've been trailing these hombres almost since we split up. Saw 'em cross our line and almost plugged 'em then, but thought I'd let 'em run and find out what they were going to do."

In a deceptively mild voice, she asked, "Or who they were coming to see?"

"Well, yeah, I reckon I've kept cases on you," Hughes admitted with chagrin. "But you ain't blaming me too awful much, I hope. When they headed your way, I got suspicioning y'all were going to meet. I didn't figure what for."

Jessie made no comment. In sultry rage she returned to taking off bridles and bits, and hanging them on the horses' saddlehorns. She was just finishing when the faint *rataplan* of hoofbeats reached them.

"More company coming," she said. "Your hands?"

"Shouldn't be, not o'er here at this hour."

The only visible indication of the riders was a flock of swallows winging restlessly from distant timber. Staring, Jessie saw another, nearer flock rise disturbed, and she commented, "They're coming, but I don't know if they're after us."

"Well, let's see if they dog our steps."

Jessie slapped the gunmen's horses on their rumps, sending them galloping in the direction of the

101

riders. Then, mounting her sorrel, she started off with Hughes at a spritely trot, heading the opposite way out of the draw. From there they threaded through timber, mostly white-bark pine and mountain hemlock, until they intercepted a meandering track where passing hoofs had beaten the ground raw. Taking the northerly trail, they crossed an area of shallow, eroded gullies with a million rabbits scampering through dead sage runnels. Beyond this open space —an old burnover, Jessie decided—they curved in along a creek, the trail flanking the bank upstream. All this time they had been alert as they rode, but there was no sign of pursuit. Once they reined in, however, and dimly heard riders behind them.

The creek-bank trail entered a pass, its floor pretty well brushed over with laurel and juniper trees. The sides of the wide pass were banked rock, pitted and honeycombed for maybe forty feet up, and above these slopes, widening back and up at a slant, it seemed to be boulders and juniper. After quite a stretch, the trail curved away from the creek-bank due to the roughness of the terrain, and it wove through an interlocking belt of wooded growth and great glazed boulders. Where the trail became crazily serpentine, Hughes slowed and glanced around, muttering there had to be a path.

There was, cutting away between two grey chunky stones—unnoticeable unless one knew where to look. Following the path, they crossed the floor and climbed the bank to a ledge, about thirty feet up in a niche of rock, screened from view by chokeberry and juniper saplings. The rock slope behind it, and towering above it, was bare and sheer.

Reaching the ledge, they removed their rifles and

picketed the horses back by a shallow cave, like a grotto, hollowed in the stone bank. At the rim of the ledge they judged the pros and cons of various spots, and crawled into a dense tier of saplings with big, waxy leaves. They lay stretched out full-length on their stomachs, their weapons before them, with a clear view of the trail below.

"This may take a while," Hughes said.

That was fine by Jessie. Now in early afternoon, the day was shirtsheeve warm, breezeless and slanting with moted sunrays under the slight canopy of foliage, lulling her with an aura of tranquility. She knew they would have to make a stand here if this didn't shake their pursuers—that is, if they hadn't lost them already, and she still had doubts whether they'd even been chased. Odds were, she figured, that nobody would come, and she'd get to enjoy some rare peace and quiet.

"This is pleasant, Long Tom, wherever we are."

"It's a campsite, on occasion, for owlhoots riding the Lechuza." Hughes pointed to the trail below. "That's where it goes. This hasn't been used much since it got gen'rally known a few years ago, when a posse cornered Stinkfinger Muldoon here. Pierce would remember it, but I don't think many of his guncrew were around then."

Jessie shifted her body, and reflexively Hughes touched her. They lay prone that way for quite a while, aware of each other and stirred by the closeness and the knowledge, until Hughes said apologetically.

"Y'know, the meanest chore a man has to do is 'fess to a tomfool mistake. Well, I'm doing it. I was wrong to've suspicioned you and what them Block-P

103

gunmen were after. I'm crow-eatin' sorry."

Jessie could feel his breath against her face and smell the fragrance of his masculine body. "Don't be sorry. They were after me, that's what, and they would've killed me if it hadn't been for you." She had long since gotten over her momentary pique; instead, now, she sensed light tendrils of arousal gradually beginning to curl in her belly and loins, against her will, and she clenched her buttocks in a futile attempt to quell them.

Hughes felt her tensing and touched her again. "I hope this does take a long time," he said with a swift surge of feeling coming into his eyes.

"Why?"

"Because it gives me an excuse to stay here and talk to you."

"That isn't what you do with other women."

"Why, sure it is."

"Not you, Long Tom. You wouldn't be satisfied just to talk to them."

Her golden-green eyes pulled half shut as she said it, and she bent her head to look at his face. Long Tom's thrusting impulse to wrap his arm around Jessie was elemental, without conscious thought or effort. It was natural as breathing. And she pressed her body against him as he kissed her on the lips. He held the kiss until her head went giddy, then relaxed his embrace and took his mouth away reluctantly, little by little.

His voice was husky. "I guess now I done you wrong the other day."

Expecting indignation, Hughes saw a veiled amusement soften the contours of her face. Her lips, ripe from kissing, eased into a slow smile and she purred, "I'm not sorry about that, either." She regarded him without reserve, her wild emotions storming out as if to smash down the code between them. She nestled close and kissed him back. "Or for that, Long Tom."

Provoked by her taunting intimacies, Hughes pressed her flat in a strong embrace. Her breasts pulsed against him through her blouse. She felt his hands move over the silken fabric, and wished he would run his fingers across her naked flesh. Yet she was aware he was still apprehensive to ask, maybe offending her, the boss lady. They continued kissing with increased fervor, passion mounting until—

"Naked," he gasped, "I want you naked. . . ."

Jessie murmured assent. "You, too."

Hughes fumbled hurriedly to skin out of his clothes. Jessie gazed at him, her lips glistening, a smoky glow in her eyes as she shucked bare and stretched out on the undergrowth, swollen breasts throbbing, curvaceous hips slackly apart, her tender self exposed invitingly.

Now also nude, Hughes eased alongside her and hovered with both hands prowling over her breasts and nipples. Jessie squirmed, sighing, his touches igniting her . . . then she shuddered as he dipped his head down to her trembling belly and tongued her navel. She whimpered, tangling her fingers in his hair, while his tongue moved farther down and thrust deep, teasing her delicate flesh and tasting her loins. Her thighs clenched spasmodically around his laving tongue and nibbling lips, excitement spiraling up in her.

Hughes eased his tongue along her cleft, swirling back and forth across her most sensitive area. Jessie

105

sucked in her breath, exhaling sharply in repsonse to his sucking mouth, spearing tongue, and nipping teeth. A minute . . . two minutes . . . her belly rippled. She began to pant explosively, her hips curving up, her pelvis grinding against his face with pulsating tension.

Jessie climaxed, wailing, twisting in the clutch of her sweet agony. She shivered, then relaxed, or *tried* to relax, as Hughes continued his savoring tongue against her moist pink flesh, and she felt herself building to another crest.

"That, that's enough . . . I'm ready. . . . Now, now . . ."

Hughes rose and knelt over her. She lay silent with anticipation, her legs bent on either side of him, her exposed center moist and throbbing. He levered downward, and she groaned with the rock-hard feel of him as he began his penetrating entry. God, how she felt it! She widened her legs, sprawling and squirming lasciviously, feeling his shaft plow deep, deep inside her tender furrow, throbbing and searching out every fold, every hidden nook and cranny.

"Migawd," she moaned, "no wonder you're called Long Tom."

Their eyes met, smiling, and he slowly began pumping. Automatically she responded in rhythm, mewing deep in her throat, her splayed thighs arching, bucking against his pistoning loins. He licked her cheek and laved her ear, then their mouths touched, pressing together with lips apart and tongues intertwining. Their tempo increased and increased again to a greedy pace, their naked flesh frantic with rutting madness. There was nothing but exquisite sensation, no existence beyond the boundaries of their bodies.

Then Jessie felt him grow even larger, saw his eyes sparkle with lust, and felt his tension and quickening race to orgasm. His bruising pummeling triggered her own release again. She sobbed as her second climax overwhelmed her, nails raking, her limbs jerking violently.

"Ahhhh . . . !"

She felt Hughes peak then, felt his juices spewing hot within. She milked all of his flowing passion until, with a last convulsion, she lay still, satiated. Then he sagged, exhausted and drained. They stretched out side by side, so she could lie with him clamped inside her, their bodies entwined as they gazed out over the ledge for signs of pursuers below, spotting nothing.

Finally, almost drowsily, she slid free of him and explained demurely, "I have to piddle." Leaving him surveying the view in a contented stupor, she flitted off toward the rear of the ledge, thinking how poorly she'd figured things: Somebody sure did come, okay, and she got to enjoy a rare if not very quiet peace.

Then she caught another sound, distant, filtering from down the trail—a faint clicking noise like that made by the beat of horses' irons on pebbly hardpan. She hastened back to the rim, shamelessly nude, her body still hot to the touch as she wedged in beside Hughes. For a long moment there were no more betraying sounds, but when they came—the jingling of metal against metal—she felt sure horses were approaching at a goodly pace.

Hughes laid some .50-90 cartridges within easy reach for his single-shot Sharps. Jessie loaded the .44

Winchester '73 she'd brought along. The beat of the irons grew louder, quickly swelling to a deep, ground-drubbing roll. They lay motionless, sighting on the trail as the first push of riders careened into view. Behind them streamed more, a looming flow of big men on big horses, as vicious and ugly-looking a half-dozen as you ever set eyes on.

Jessie stared grimly, prepared to empty a saddle or two should any of them chance to see them up here. Luckily, the gunmen neglected to check along the sides. They focused on the way ahead as they swept around the curves and on up out of sight, in the direction of the Lechuza Trail.

"We'll have to wait some more," Hughes said, as the low drumming pound of their passage was fading. "Have to be sure they don't stop or double back."

"And are you hoping it'll be long, so you can talk to me some more?"

"I think there's a hard point we ought to get straight between us."

"Feel up to it?" Jessie teased, then gasped, "Lord, do you!"

His virile manhood was regaining hardness and girth. Despite being fulfilled and aching, Jessie found that her loins were responding, pushing upward, clasping his resurgent shaft as he entered and swallowing his full, thick length inside her yearning belly. She closed her eyes, feeling an erotic blaze rekindling between her thighs. . . .

Along about the time Jessie was encountering the three gunmen, Ki was riding down Unity's main street. He too was enjoying the pleasant day, but more out of a sense of relief, for it indicated tonight would be clear and moonlit, allowing him more time to locate the hidden gold. Yet he also was aware that these were the days of quick storms and rain squalls, as well as spells of bright sun. And on the northwestern horizon, there seemed to be a suspicious gray edging like a stagnant scum line.

The sheriff's substation looked dim and empty inside as Ki passed on his way to the livery. Returning on foot, however, he spotted Deputy Voight at a table near the window of a restaurant, a hole in the wall called the Mecca Cafe. Voight was gazing out the window as he ate, and gestured for Ki to join him.

Ki had a cup of coffee with him.

"Well, I likely won't get another stab at respectable chow till I get back tomorrow sometime, maybe late," Voight remarked, plowing through a mounded platter of porkchops, wild greens, and little bullet-shaped yams. He took out of his pocket a folded circular such as are sent out by sheriffs' offices and police agencies. Handing it to Ki, he said, "This came in from Butte County, down in the northern gold country."

Ki unfolded the circular and studied the scowling, hard-eyed face depicted. Below the likeness he read:

MAYHEW Q(UINCY) KNAUB
SUSPICION OF MURDER & ARMED ROBBERY

MAYHEW KNAUB, LATELY EMPLOYED AS DRIFT FOREMAN AT CORONADO MINE, LOCHINVAR, CALIFORNIA. UNACCOUNTABLY MISSING FROM WORK AND HABITATION. SUSPECTED OF COMPLICITY IN ARMED ROBBERY OF CORONADO

MINE GOLD SHIPMENT VALUED AT ONE HUNDRED THOUSAND DOLLARS, DURING THE COMMISSION OF WHICH A STAGE DRIVER AND TWO GUARDS WERE SHOT DEAD.

A description of Knaub followed, then a notice of reward from Coronado, and then the addresses of the Coronado and the sheriff's station at Oroville. Ki glanced up to meet Voight's gaze.

"It's him, okay," Voight declared. "The short, husky one with the gray hair, the one that wore the laced boots. A hundred grand. Damnation! That's a deep pocketful of gold."

"Coronado seems to think so," Ki commented. "They're offering five thousand bucks for its return, and another thousand for the capture and conviction of the robbers. I'd venture those four dead 'uns were the four who pulled that job."

"But where's the gold?"

"That's the question." Ki grinned. "Shrewd, weren't they? Didn't head for Mexico, as everybody'd think they would. Took a chance and hit the Lechuza Trail, figuring if they could just get a head start, they'd do okay. The Lechuza doesn't run through any towns, so while the posses were combing the country to the south and east, they were heading toward the Northwest and Canada. But it appears they ran into a trouble at the M-Over-Y."

"And it also appears that Yokum McQuade ran into a pack of good luck," Voight added dourly. "I don't reckon anyone hereabouts will get a chance to ask Yokum any questions."

"Probably not."

"But Thad Ingersoll is askin' questions and supplyin' his own answers," Voight went on disgustedly. "Ingersoll is toutin' that the gold was there at the M-Over-Y when you and Miss Starbuck rode in, and that maybe Angus was there, too, and had kind of vanished when me and my troop arrived."

"Meaning the two of us did away with McQuade, and the gold, too."

"Pretty much so. Do you care to deny it?"

"I don't care to even answer it." Ki sat stewing thoughtfully for a moment, then said, "I may need you in a hurry soon."

"Doesn't everybody," Voight sighed. "Had a hectic morning, and now I'm late gettin' goin' out to serve a hill farmer with a bastardy paper. Then I have to ride way over to the Givler homestead. Last night some drunken Block-P boys filched all their horses, 'cept a decrepit buggy mare, and later Pierce came offerin' to buy 'em. For match sticks and cigar ends, accordin' to Givler."

"Is Pierce after their land?"

"No, and he has no want of horses. No doubt a rowdy prank, and he'll have returned 'em before I show up. He better. I don't coddle nag-nappers."

"No doubt," Ki said, rising to leave. "If I send for you, don't ask and don't tell; just come, quick as you can. Okay?"

"I'll do it. You messing amok on your own is something my peace-lovin' mind dreads to ponder," Voight said. When Ki turned toward the door, he added casually, "Stay out of the Esquire."

"Why?"

"Wahoo Delgardo and sundry hands are in there."

"With the Givler horses?"

"With my opinion of that horseplay boilin' their

booze. They're tetchy and mean, and fast wor-senin'," Voight said. "So always remember one thing."

"What's that?"

"A soft answer—not a hand-forged bowie knife —turneth away wrath."

"Oh, I wouldn't forget that. No, sir. Not that," Ki said gravely, and headed for the street and the Es-quire Saloon.

Chapter 9

It was the shank of the afternoon when Jessie and Long Tom Hughes returned to the Anvil ranchstead. A half-hour after they'd stabled their horses, the Anvil ranch wagon arrived back from town, drawn rattling by a lathery bayard at a whip-rousing lope. The driver brought it lurching to a halt before the bunkhouse, followed by Rawhide and a scattering of cowhands coming on the run. Rawhide was among the first to reach the wagon.

The driver was a veteran cowhand, knotty, tough of sinew, now haggard and wild-voiced as he broke the news to Rawhide. The others were gathering round, Jessie and Hughes joining as the driver was saying, "... Voight not in, nor Doc Lozier. We parked out of sight and I checked around town for 'em. Gresham stayed with the wagon, guarding the

113

bodies. Somehow Block-P caught onto him there, as you can see."

Rawhide could see. Everyone could, and it was not a pretty sight.

Gresham, who'd accompanied the driver as his helper, was a strapping boy about sixteen, all cowpoke and no nonsense. Dazed, he groped and crawled on his hands and knees in the wagonbed, struggling to his feet now that the wagon was still, refusing the outstretched help of his bunkmates. His face, if it could be called a face, was red, pulpy, and half toothless.

"I'sh aw'ri," Gresham slurred, and fell out of the wagon.

A couple of hands caught him. One said. "We'll put him in his bunk."

A third volunteered, "Lemme try an' find the doc."

"Doc was seen taking the noon stage to Klamath Falls for supplies," the driver said. "He'll be back late tomorrow, like as not, about the same time as Dep'ty Voight is expected in from *his* trip."

Rawhide said, "Duey, go fetch Toledo from the west basin."

Nodding, the volunteer sped off for a horse.

Bleak-eyed, Rawhide glanced from Duey to the two cowhands who were half carrying, half dragging Gresham into the bunkhouse. He said to the driver, "I was afeared of this, Everett, specially since you got so overdue returnin'. I was wrong to've risked you agin' the Block-P like I did."

"Beggin' your pardon, boss, but that's where you an' Miz Jessie were right on the bean," Everett countered. "The Block-P ain't what delayed us. On our way in, that faulty wheel hub loosened again, and we nearly lost the axle—cap, pad and collar. But in town, Wahoo brung enough men to cause trouble for any sizable bunch we'd have mustered. Just me an' Gresham, we had no problem going roundaback quick and quiet. If we hadn't had to repair the hub, we'd have seen Dep'ty Voight, and he'd have seen the Block-P stiff. Like you said, maybe that wouldn't have convinced him, but I betcha he'd be here now, taking our side of things more seriously."

"Yeah? Wal, what become of the bodies?"

"Block-P snatched 'em. They were gone when I got back to the wagon. Gresham was pistol-whipped senseless, and Block-P'ers caught me in a trap. Wahoo bragged he'd swap the bodies for mine and Gresham's, claiming we'd be an even trade," Everett growled. "He would've, too, 'cept for Miz Jessie's amigo coming out of nowhere."

"Ki?" Jessie gasped.

"Yes'm, that's who. They had me ringed in, guns held pistol-whip style, as Wahoo swung first at me with my own gun. Out of nowhere, Ki come an' swung Wahoo hisself, arse over spurs, into his own men. Ki got my gun away from him as he was flinging, and wheeled from man to man, clubbin' their faces with steel. The noise, migawd, the howlin', the cussin'!" Everett shook his head wonderously. "Some rallied with Wahoo to gang-rush him. Ki didn't kill 'em, but next thing to it, maiming, crippling, busting bones and messing ugly wolves uglier. They wound up sprawling in a heap, Wahoo knocked breathless on the bottom."

"What?" Hughes guffawed. "Ki tuckered a mob of Block-P hardcases?"

Everett nodded. "And so fast, I couldn't give you a blow by blow. That ain't the end of it. Whilst they're all downed moanin' and wrigglin', Ki put Gresham in the wagon and told me to get the hell gone, that it was vital I get back here and give Miz Jessie this—." Everett swept off his crumpled hat— "then Ki run off and stampeded their horses hidden back in the brush. He was riding one as they bolted out 'pon the Block-P'ers. Men scrambled, horses scattered, I larruped away from there to here."

"Why does Ki want me to have your hat?" Jessie wondered.

"Can't say that he does," Everett replied, taking from the hat's inner sweatband a wadded, torn strip of newspaper. "All he told me was to safekeep this note to you."

The message was penciled in blunt block letters along the narrow margin, indicating Ki had been in a hurry, using whatever he found at hand. It read:

AM IN STOREROOM, ESQUIRE SALOON. OVER-HEARD BLOCK-P GANG INTENDING TO MAKE UP FOR LAST NIGHT WITH MORE OF THEM—AP-PROX. TWO DOZEN—AND LESS OF ANVIL BY CRIPPLING HOWEVER MANY OF YOU RIDE TO GET VOIGHT. ONE OF THE TOWN BARFLIES JUST IN, REPORTS ANVIL WAGON TURNING UP BY SMOKEHOUSE BEHIND BUTCHER SHOP. BLOCK-P LEAVING TO SEE, ALSO SOMETHING TO DO ABOUT CORPSES(?) I'LL FOLLOW, DO WHAT I CAN TO HASH THINGS UP AND GET THIS TO YOU. DON'T TRY FOR VOIGHT, HE'S LURED OUT OF TOWN OVERNIGHT. DON'T SPLIT FORCES. DO EX-PECT TROUBLE ANY TIME.

Jessie handed it to Rawhide. Over his shoulder Hughes scanned the note, then angrily turned to his men, ordering: "Fetch everybody in, pronto!"

Soon a council of war developed, the Anvil crew arguing and fussing what should be done.

"Boss," Long Tom Hughes exclaimed at last, "There's only one thing to do, as I sees it. Let's take the play away from Pierce, the skunk! We'll cross him, see! We'll ride over, and burn every stick on his place!"

There were grunts of approval. But Rawhide shook his head.

"Sounds good, Long Tom, just like it did about a bunch of us parading in to see the law," Rawhide told his foreman. "It works bad for the same reason. Pierce has too many men. His buildings are better protected. Sure, I got *better* men—" Rawhide grinned fleetingly at his crew— "but not so many of 'em. No, we got to stay here and try to protect ourselves; we can't stand any more losses. But we got our work cut out!"

"We have one advantage," Jessie said thoughtfully. "Pierce must think he'll surprise us, get the jump. But we know he's coming, no doubt heading for the main house, and look how he'll have to come. The trail leads in through that batch of sheds and utility outbuildings, then curves around the front yard by the stable barn, loops up near the main house, swerves once more, and ends at the wagonshed next to the blacksmith shanty." Jessie pointed out the route as she explained, concluding, "Some of you boys can catch the Block-P from the side. We'll be in the house, throwing them off balance. The rest of you rush in from behind, or from behind the creek

117

bank ahead, full speed, as soon as you hear the first shot. We'll ambush them in a crossfire. Got it?"

"Yes, we got it," Long Tom said slowly, "and it looks pretty good."

Rawhide cackled maliciously. "If we do lose, by cracky, there won't be much left, and Pierce can have it—if he can foreclose from Hell."

The crew was positioned with great care, along the lines Jessie had proposed. Rawhide insisted on personally signaling the counterattack from front and rear and, armed with his distinctive-sounding Peabody .45/70/480 rimfire rifle, he took up a dangerously exposed observation point at the corrals. Hughes considered a cowhand named Unruh to be the best marksman of the lot; Jessie stationed Unruh with his old Kentucky squirrel rifle in the outside cellar, where he could cover the broad, flat sweep of the lane before the porch. Jessie posted herself, along with Hughes and Everett, in the front parlor of the house; lit a few lamps; added green wood to the kitchen stove fire to make it smoke cheerily; and sent Bertha off to visit a sister. The house would be the focus of the attack.

Then they waited.

Gradually the sun set. There was a saffron interval when the world glowed dully, when long shadows stretched out from posts and sheds, and then the glow was gone, leaving only an unnatural twilight, a watery, colorless stain. There was neither movement of air, nor sound.

Block-P came in that moment of half-light. As the first blotting shadows of night, like vague purple fists, were groping outward from the encircling walls, they launched themselves down the slope;

118

twenty riders, with a thunder of hoofs, single-file, at full gallop, fetlocks and iron horseshoes bruising the hardpan of the wagon lane.

They were picked men, obviously. Some were known to Rawhide; some were feverish, eager strangers. The 'breed was among them, Jessie saw. Wahoo Delgardo was in the lead, but there was no sign of Felix Pierce himself.

Down in a rush they came, pounding along the lane between the sheds, into the ranchyard, deploying about the house, flinging themselves from their saddles. This was the instant that Jessie had set for action, and from the house and barn, blazing at precisely the right moment, roared salvoes of gunfire. Two men went down under their fire, one knocked over in the act of running toward the house, the other slammed from his saddle. Again and again blasted the venomous rifles of the defenders; a third Pierce man went down with a fractured knee, and a fourth stood foolishly with a broken arm. Somewhere along the line, Rawhide had let fly with his Peabody, and from the shelter of sheds and the creek bank, the balance of Anvil cowhands joined in the murderous crossfire.

In the flick of that sequence of seconds, the yard became a howling, rattling bedlam. The yells that rang out carried confusion and alarm. Some of the raiders were still mounted, some on the ground and running aimlessly, some still in the act of swinging from their stirrups. Shots seemed to be coming at them from everywhere. They knew they were trapped, but were unable to judge the strength of their opposition. They wavered, indecisive, on the verge of panic.

But Wahoo was fighting back, determined to reorganize and stabilize the Block-P forces. Like a madman, he was kicking, pulling, shrieking, and waving. He was pointing, too, to the barn, the cellar, the house, and over at Rawhide hunkering by the corral fence. Men began following his advice, forming small orderly parties, storming the targets he indicated.

Jessie, standing within her window, slipped on one of her empty cartridge cases. Regaining her balance, she broke out another glass pane for unhampered shooting, glimpsing Rawhide rallying his Anvil hands to meet the challenge. A Block-P raider, his gun shot out of his hand by an Anvil man, came at Rawhide with a long, razor-sharp knife. He got to within a foot of the ranch-owner; the heavy blade sliced down. Then, abruptly, his face went blank; between his eyes there appeared suddenly a round hole, with bluish edges.

Jessie levered her Winchester for another shot, but the magazine was empty. Hastily she started thumbing fresh loads into her rifle, horrified to see another Pierce killer lunge unnoticed at Rawhide.

"Rawhide!"

He could not possibly hear her, but as though he had, Rawhide turned then and saw his enemy. He flung up his gun hand. At that same instant, or a little in advance, the Block-P man fired his revolver. Rawhide swayed, fell forward. The Block-P men rallied by this tragedy, swept toward the house over the spot where he had been.

Jessie and Hughes, and Everett across from them, opened up full blast, lining their shots at the saffron flares that were winking in the dimness outside.

120

Through the racket, Jessie was able to hear Wahoo hurling curses and goading his men. The parlor began to reek with choking fumes, and a fog of powder smoke thickened down from the ceiling. Lead chewed constantly into the walls and through the windows, zipping and ricocheting about the room, as Block-P men bellied in from the sides and across the dim yard.

"Rush 'em!" Wahoo was commanding, still out there, no slouch when it came to fighting. "C'mon, you lazy bastards!"

But the trio trapped inside kept his advancing gunhands respectful with swift, accurate fire. A man scurrying by Jessie's window abruptly let out a cry and clawed at his chest, spurting blood on his calf-skin vest. Hughes rammed his Sharps out his window, and as its thunderous discharge receded, wails and thrashing could be heard from outside. Everett muttered as he worked his rifle, while the continuous *slam-slam* of weapons could be heard coming from the barn and sheds, and from the direction of the creek.

Gunmen charged the house, but bullets, crying in a steady whine, drove them back. Twice more it looked as if the defenders inside were on the red road to Hell. Three gunmen managed to reach the protection of the porch. At a signal from Jessie, Everett flung open the front door; the porch outside seemed to tremble under the pounding of boots. The gunmen were rushing the doorway as though they thought a miracle had just occurred.

The first gunman to loom in the doorway had his chest demolished and half his jaw knocked off by Jessie and Hughes' lancing slugs. Another, twisting

121

in from one side, had his hat punctured in a couple of places, and dropped to a prayerlike position, tripping the third man behind. Everett shot that man in his ugly mouth, then slammed the door shut.

A fourth gunman racing to join the three, witnessed the carnage and hesitated—before scrambling out of the way. Two more followed as they saw their fast-mounting casualties sinking around them, and the attack faltered. Muddled, frantic, the Block-P survivors fell back, blundering into each other. Again there was one of the periods of indecision upon which Jessie had built her hopes.

And again Wahoo was exhorting his men, reversing the battle back in his favor. Already, as Jessie watched, men appeared with armfuls of desiccated shingles ripped from the blacksmith shanty. They were going to burn Anvil out.

This thing had to be stopped, if only for a moment—it had to be thrown once more into confusion. Carrying her Winchester, Jessie walked from the parlor, out onto the body-laden porch. She opened her mouth to shout, but there was no need. Everyone seemed to see her at once.

Hell broke loose around her. A hail of wild shots sparkled at her from the yard. The carbine was slapped from her hand by flying lead, and the porch pillars on either side of her shoulders became pocked with little wisps of toothpick-sized splinters. The greatest howl of all came from Wahoo, who responded in insensate fury, charging across the yard.

To Jessie's right, Unruh came out of his cellar. An early moon hung low in the sky, and in the blue and silver of its light, Unruh seemed a pitifully slight figure, a small slim bundle of workclothes. The movement caught Wahoo's attention. For the briefest of instants, his eyes flicked toward Unruh.

Jessie drew her pistol and nailed Wahoo three times with a smokehouse pattern. If you heard someone fooling around your smokehouse at night, and you went to the back door and could see nothing because of the dark, you placed, to your best judgment, three shots around the padlock—one above it, two more farther down, left and right, forming a triangle. It was a hard pattern to escape, even when you were shooting blind. Wahoo Delgardo shuddered and went down as though boneless, dead before the third slug hit him.

A moment of paralysis followed; then there was a flash of action down by the barn. The 'breed, half squatting, half prone, between the legs of a dead horse, using its body as protection, was preparing a torch. He had whittled a bundle of shingle splinters, tied them with a length of wire, and was about to toss it on the barn roof when Wahoo fell.

In the interval of shock, the 'breed had crooked his head around and stared at Wahoo and the house and Jessie. Now he returned his gaze to the barn. A figure, belly-crawling across the earth toward him, rose up in the gloom and shot him. That was how the 'breed died. Unruh shot him with his .50 squirrel rifle at a couple dozen feet. Squarely, as it was later discovered, through the crown of the head, down through the flesh of the throat, and into the chest.

It was then that M-Over-Y galloped in.

They attacked in their own fashion, from down along the creek bank and in a fan across the yard, hurrawing their horses, their weapons in the air, as though it were a month-end skylark. They struck the

Block-P'ers on their flank, and five went down under the initial charge.

It was an awesome marvel to behold. Jud Grampus, looking righteously indignant, was yelling complicated curses. Orville Hicks was stone-faced, implacable, letting his pistol do all the talking. Latigo Doyle was having the time of his life; as good a time almost, Jessie decided, as if he were busting up a saloon. Ki was bearing down low in the saddle, slashing right and left with a cavalry saber, which Jessie presumed must belong to Yokum McQuade.

Leaderless now, the Block-P men faltered. Professional killers, they knew their job but they were befogged by confusion. And from their unprotected flank, they were being shot to shreds by three men, while a fourth sliced their arms and chests, hacked heads and spinal cords. Panic seized them. They ran helter-skelter, grabbing for uninjured horses. Some ended on the ground. Others had their horses shot out from under them, and clung to the stirrups of those still mounted. Few, if any, managed to live through it unscathed, as they thundered out on the wagon trail, beating a retreat as fast as they could gallop, speeding on their way with blistering gun volleys. The *rataplan* of clicking irons faded swiftly in the distance.

The M-Over-Y did not attempt pursuit, but stayed to help Anvil in the aftermath, taking stock of the damage already done. The ranch hands groaned and groused, for the gun fray had left them all aching with countless scratches, contusions, nicks and bruises. It also caused numerous sprains and chipped bones and minor bullet creases. Only two suffered serious injuries—a left ear shot off, and a bullet hole through a left thigh—but four had died, though they had taken with them almost three times that many Block-P raiders.

First thing to be seen to, however, was Rawhide. He lay supine on the crusty earth by the corral fence, one arm above his head, his eyes closed, a big wet blotch of blood below his upper shoulder. The wound looked bad to Jessie, as she got to her knees; it really must have hammered him when the slug hit. She placed her ear against his chest.

"He shouldn't be," she said, "but he's still breathing."

Opening his eyes, Rawhide looked at her unseeingly. "Of course I'm breathing," he whispered hoarsely, closing his eyes. "That's all I can do right now."

Hughes was flabbergasted. "Can't be! You're shot dead!"

"I sure's hell will be, you nincompoop, if you don't get me patched up," Rawhide said. In his exasperation, a fleck of bloody foam gathered at the corner of his lip.

Hurriedly, a large blanket was brought. Then four men, each holding a corner, carried Rawhide hammock-style into the house. Jessie went on ahead to prepare his bed and ease him under the covers.

A few steps behind came the cowhand named Toledo. He was youngish, with round fish eyes and a jaw like a block of grindstone, and he quickly showed Jessie why Rawhide had wanted him fetched for Gresham. Toledo had a knack for doctoring, and though he'd never been schooled, he examined Rawhide's wound with more skill than many a medico Jessie had seen.

When he was done, he said, "Boss, you're not

hurt too awful. It went clean through your withers but missed the bone. I'll write a note to take to the druggist. Don't push y'self and you oughta heal okay."

Beside Toledo, Jessie watched him write rapidly on piece of paper: *Gum benzoin in powder, balsam of tolu in powder, gum storax, frankincense, myrrh, aloe in quantities by the ounce, and alcohol 1 gal. To be applied externally for wounds, taken internally for pain.*

"Why, that's horse medicine," Jessie said, "for horse wounds!"

"We're all God's creatures," Toledo said. "It's highly reliable. I always use it myself."

And hundreds of doctors and ranchers used it too, and swore by it, Jessie knew. She shut up. A wound was a wound.

Hours later, when the dead were buried and the wounded were tended and resting, Long Tom Hughes came upon Ki out on the porch, contemplating the now peaceful, moonlit yard. Joining him, Hughes lighted a black, crooked cigar and smoked quietly for a few moments, gazing out at the spectral scene of silver and shadow.

Finally he commented, "I don't think Miss Jessie is much afraid of Felix Pierce or his Block-P."

"No, probably she isn't."

"I don't think she's much afraid of anybody, ever."

"I used to be that way," Ki remarked. "But things changed and I got older and wiser and sadder. And downright cowardly. You ought to try it."

"Do you have to work at it, or did your talent come natural-born?"

"Practice and dedication. Be careful to bother no-body so nobody bothers you. You live in a state of bliss."

"So that's how you get cowardly," Hughes said admiringly. "You sure make it sound appetizin'. But just the same, Ki, I'm glad you had a lapse from grace and brung your boys in when you did. We're beholden to you, we are."

"You're liable to be asked to honor that debt before long," Ki replied enigmatically, "and to help collect a few overdue ones."

Hughes frowned quizzically, but Ki did not see fit to elaborate farther right then. The time would come, though; it was fast approaching.

Chapter 10

Under a midnight moon, Ki and his crew returned to the M-Over-Y.

The following day started out crystal clear, with crisp, tangy autumn air, and amethyst and rose sunlight. Ki and Latigo Doyle started out working the south range, the range nearest the ranch house, but also the toughest. Box canyons, dry washes, narrow ravines, and scrambled ridges were jumbled together; but maverick steers hid in the watered canyons and fed on the flowering weeds that speckled the sides of the washes.

Ki and Latigo spent a busy morning and turned homeward at noon with a gathering of strays that justified their efforts.

Suddenly Latigo rose in the stirrups, pointing his forefinger. "Look, o'er there, by the scrub oak. There's a hoss and it seems in sorrowful shape."

They turned their mounts, and the tired cattle took advantage of the respite to graze on nearby grass. The horse was a piebald brute of a stallion and was truly ailing, hardly able to move because of deep sores just back of its withers.

"Saddle galls," Latigo grunted, "but hell, what a load the poor critter must've been carryin' to get that way! Saddlebags must've been packed with lead!"

"I've got some ointment in my pouch," Ki remarked, a peculiar light in his dark eyes. "At least it'll ease the pain and keep the flies from laying eggs in the open sores."

As Ki was procuring the ointment, Latigo gave an exclamation. He was staring at the brand on the piebald's haunch. "'Cross in a Box,'" he read. "Now what kind o' ringer is that? There ain't no Cross in a Box spread anywheres in this section."

"D'you know of one anywhere at all?"

"Wal . . . I think I rec'lect spottin' that brand down a ways in nor'eastern Sacramento Valley, but I'd hate to swear to it," Latigo said, as they applied the soothing ointment to the sores. "Reckon some hellion what had oughta have his throat slit rode up here and set the big feller loose when he got sore. I hope that hydrophobic rat has sores like these to sit on!"

"A horse this lame would hardly move from where it was left," Ki murmured, scanning the terrain. And that, he reckoned, was how a man who didn't know much about horses may've slipped badly. Yet time was tight, he reminded himself, glancing skyward. The heavens had lost their earlier clarity and were turning preternaturally blue, with a single faraway cloud of sluggish gray, like a vaporous sheet of dirty muslin, creeping in from the north-west.

"Y'know, Latigo, we largely cleaned out the south range this morning," Ki asserted zestfully. "So instead of wasting time back there after lunch, maybe you should go work with Grampus and Hicks on the north range."

That was hunky-dory with Latigo. And notwithstanding his talk, the afternoon found Ki back in the locality where they had encountered the stricken piebald. He reined in by a meandering creek and let his black nuzzle the water gratefully as he watched the encroaching overcast and wondered if he could backtrack the piebald in the short time remaining. The piebald, he reasoned, would not—could not—have crossed the creek, so it must've been set loose on this side. It'd have made for water, the closest it could find, and it'd have tried to travel downhill. So probably it'd wandered from one of those canyons or washes to the southeast. Question was, which one? If it hadn't rained so hard and so long, there might have been some tracks. As it was, he'd just have to do some hard looking.

On into the afternoon, Ki diligently combed the canyon and wash, passing by those spots which contained water, for he felt confident the sore piebald wouldn't have strayed from such a place. During the hours the lip of the overcast grew, accumulating gradually and so lifelessly that its growth was almost imperceptible. The moisture started in mid-afternoon, seeming to come with no fall, but simply to materialize about the same time Ki noted his first encouraging sign. Where a heavy cluster of overhanging branches had somewhat deflected the down-

131

pour, was a deeply scored hoofmark, a mark that pointed *up* the canyon.

Ki studied it with care. The horse making that mark was carrying a heavy load, he could readily see; but he couldn't tell if it'd been the piebald, or one of the other three that hadn't been seen hide or hair of all this while. Of course, the others may've been in good shape to travel and were run off somewhere. Ki felt there was a good chance of that.

He came upon a crevice, really little more than a crack, a narrow box canyon that squeezed even narrower as it bored into the hills. Ki rode slowly, exploring the ground with attentive eyes.

A second deeply scored print at the base of an overhanging rock brought a lean, mirthless grin to his lips. Then the canyon petered out to a slender slit that ended against a lofty wall, with equally tall perpendicular walls on either hand. Frustrated, irritated, Ki turned back. But now he gave his attention to the side walls of the canyon and the thick, hardy growth that bristled up and out like unkempt hedgerows along the base of the cliffs.

He was halfway down the canyon when a clump of brush caught his eye. It was an evergreen growth, but the shiny leaves had a dull and grayish tint different from other bushes of the same type, including one growing right next to it.

Turning his horse, he drifted closer and found his answer. The leaves were wilted. Dismounting, Ki wormed his way under the bush and found that the stout trunk, instead of being naturally rooted in the ground, was thrust into a crevice between two stones. The bush had been cut, dragged over and

132

posted on this spot . . . only this time, somebody forgot to relieve his post, Ki suspected.

He started to haul the bush from its crevice, then abruptly changed his mind. Instead, he carefully worked his way under and around the prickly bristle, wincing at the bite of the thorns, but refraining from breaking branch or twig. Finally Ki made it, at the expense of a little skin, and stood staring at a dark opening in the face of the cliff. He crept closer and peered within.

It was the mouth of a cave, extending an unguessable distance into the canyon wall. Ki considered a moment, then turned and pushed his way along the face of the cliff. In a shallow dry wash he found an abundance of dried sotol stalks which could serve as torches in a pinch. Securing several, he returned to the cave mouth. There he lighted one and entered the narrow passage.

There was barely room for him to stand erect at first, but after a few feet the roof lifted and the walls fell back. Another moment and he was in a wide, earth-floored cavern whose extent he could not estimate. He was but a few yards from one wall, the light of the torch disclosed, but the other was shrouded in darkness. He stepped across, holding his torch high, and found that both walls were irregularly cut, with juts of stone, and shallow recesses.

Before one of these recesses he paused, peering at the unmistakable evidence of freshly turned earth. He fingered the hilt of the largest knife he carried, his *tanto,* but decided it was hardly suitable for digging. It was not far to the mouth of the cave, however, and Ki hurried out and found a stout trunk with a number of branches forking out in a cluster.

He hacked the bush off close to the ground and cut and trimmed the branches until he had what would pass for a spade. With this he returned to the cave and went to work. Removing the earth, which had been packed and tamped, was a tough job but he persisted and soon hit a yielding object. Another half hour and he had uncovered a stout leather saddlebag which taxed his strength to drag from the hole. It clanked dully as he drew it forth.

Undoing the buckle flap, Ki peered inside. The torch light reflected a yellowish gleam. Gold ingots. This was the cache, all right.

Prodding with the makeshift spade met with the same yielding resistance, which convinced Ki that other saddlebags containing ingots lay in the shallow hole. Grim-faced, then, he turned to another spot which bore the signs of recent excavation—a long, narrow rectangle. Here he dug with the greatest care, shoveling the loose earth with his hands. Finally he stared into a marred and distorted face crowned by a thatch of grizzled hair. A little more digging uncovered a gray flannel shirt blotched with dark and ominous stains.

Kneeling, Ki checked the corpse to confirm his suspicions, then stood and stared down at the pitiful remains a moment, thinking: Knifed in the back, all right, between the shoulder blades. By an expert, at that, a true killer artist, able to throw from darkness at a difficult angle, and skewer his victim's heart through the back.

Face bleak, eyes cold as windswept glaciers, Ki reverently replaced the disturbed earth. He reburied the bag of gold as well, patting and smoothing the spot until a casual glance would fail to show evidence of an intruder.

"Just in case there might be a slip-up," he muttered, as he headed for his horse.

The drizzly overcast continued to roll darker, misting the cool sunset as Ki rode swiftly toward the M-Over-Y ranchstead. He scanned the ominous sky with satisfaction, thinking this would be the kind of night certain lobos had been waiting for.

Dusk was falling and the ranchland about him was fast becoming a murky half-world when Ki arrived and stabled his horse. Ten minutues later, Orville Hicks was riding with all speed to Unity, and Jud Grampus was setting out for the Anvil. Beth Wyndam was furious, for she had just finished preparing a huge dinner of short-ribs cooked with whole onions, mashed potatoes with short-rib gravy, and hot pumpkin bread with strained honey. She was angered all the more by Ki refusing to explain the emergency, and staying only long enough to gobble a quick bite and tell Latigo to fort up with Beth in the house. Latigo gave Ki a woebegone look, as though his order was tantamount to being locked in a lion's den with an enraged man-killer.

Ki made a few swift preparations, then wrapped a bundle of oil-soaked waste into a poncho and strapped it behind his saddle. A sodden blanket covered the moon and stars, and there was still a misty drizzle in the air, not quite vapor, not quite rain, as Ki rode out into the night. His shirt became soggy on his back, but he left his slicker rolled on the cantle; with the possibility of sudden violence as distinct as it was, he wanted no cumbersome wrap hindering his movement.

135

Ki paused where the M-Over-Y trail intersected the wagon road to Unity, then sought shelter within a bordering copse of trees. And waited. And waited some more. The overcast made it difficult to judge time, but Ki was long past feeling it had gotten good and goddamn late when he heard the rapid approach of horses.

The black outlines of seven riders loomed indistinctly along the wagon road. Ki stayed put, hand over the muzzle of his horse, watching the riders draw near the fork and rein in. After a few minutes he could hear muttering break out, and finally a familiar voice impatiently snapped, "Okay, Jud, where is he? I'm soakin' cold!"

Before Grampus could find an answer, Ki called, "Over here, Long Tom."

The seven rode across and dismounted in the copse, ground-reining their horses. As they gathered around, a glum Jud Grampus said, "Sorry, Ki."

"It's okay," Ki said, but it wasn't.

"Anyway, I tried. I'd have been here lots sooner with Miz Jessie and Long Tom, just 'em two like you wanted, 'cept everybody else insisted on tagging along. I couldn't stop 'em short of not coming myself."

"Sure, we wanted to," Long Tom said. "We was ordered to, too."

Ki glanced at Jessie.

"Don't look at me in that tone of voice," Jessie snapped. "Rawhide was convinced you'd need more than two, and ordered anyone able to seat a horse to go. It was all I could do to keep him from getting up and leading the charge."

Ki nodded, understanding but not liking it. Aside

from Jessie, Long Tom Hughes and Grampus, he recognized Everett, Deadshot Unruh, a squat, hairy ranchhand named Finch, and, incredibly, the pistol-whipped Gresham, his features obscured by deep shadow—though Ki recalled how he had looked, and knew the young cowpoke must have made this ride maddened with pain, driven by vengeance. These were good men, part of a good crew, red-tan and tough and leathery and Ki wasn't displeased to see them. He just wasn't pleased to see them here, thinking they ought to've stayed on guard at the Anvil, instead of leaving it defended by a handful of casualties.

"I go along with Rawhide on this," Hughes replied, when Ki voiced his thoughts. "We know worse is yet to come, and we'll be ready. But there's no immediate fear of another Block-P raid until Pierce scrounges more gunmen."

Listening, Jessie remembered what Long Tom had told her about the Block-P owner, and she suspected that Pierce had the contacts and money to buy a gang of cutthroats overnight. But it was futile to speculate on that here. And now memories rose of her father's frustrated efforts to help Rawhide, as she heard the Anvil foreman telling Ki:

"Rawhide Avalon is the kind of mortal man that don't like to be beholden to nobody. None of his crew do either. Upshot is, the M-Over-Y ain't paying our scores for us. We got a right, a goddamn duty, to be in on your troubles, and every man-jack here is itching to l'arn your enemies as hard a lesson as y'all drilled into Block-P. Well? What're we waiting for?"

"Deputy Voight," Ki said. "He's late."

Declaring, "That's how I stay healthy," Deputy Voight materialized in their midst.

"You came through. Thanks," Ki said earnestly. "Where's Hicks?"

"Orville Hicks? I thought he was working here. Why, you lose him?"

"I sent Hicks to your office with word to meet us here."

"Well, I no sooner got in than I had to go out again," Voight explained. "Likely our paths just missed crossing a time or few."

Ki dispatched Jud Grampus to fetch Hicks back to the ranch. Then he asked Voight, "How'd you happen to show up, like a gift from God?"

"I looked for you," Voight replied. "I'm a deputy. That's my trade."

Long Tom spoke up, sharply, "He must've follered us, that's what."

Shrugging it off, Voight announced, "Cayuse Sumpter, and Max Sunderlund of Block-P, have been found murdered."

Bewildered, Everett began blurting, "How could—"

"Why, I don't believe it!" Ki exclaimed, squelching Everett, and turned to Jessie. "I have never seen such a place for gunfights."

"This wasn't no gunfight," Voight said. "Not lest they shot 'emselves to pieces after they was dead, leavin' no blood, with nobody hearing 'em, and then —*then!*—made 'emselves comfy in Doc Lozier's locked office. His housekeeper, the Widder Blevinson, found 'em and she's still a-squallin'."

"Why talk to me about it?" Ki asked.

"I want to know if you did it."

138

Ki looked shocked. "Do you think that'd be my style?"

"Let me put it this way: I know nobody else who'd have the ba—er, gall to pull such a stunt."

Now Ki looked blank.

"You going to arrest him?" Jessie asked.

"No," Voight said, "I ain't going to arrest him. Whether I'd like to or not is somethin' else again." He fumbled through his pockets, searching, and at last came out with three papers. "But speakin' of arrest, I forthwith and hereby serve these here warrants, signed by Mr. Felix Pierce in person, to Mr. Hughes for stealing Block-P chickens, Mr. Everett for loud and abusive language, and Mr. Gresham for public nuisance."

They were outraged.

"I never stole a chicken in my life," Hughes protested. "Loud and abusive lingo I've been guilty of, and even public nuisance maybe, but not fowl-pilferin'."

"Come along," Voight ordered. "You'll have your day in court."

"We'll have a month in jail awaitin' court," Everett retorted, digging in his heels. "That's the whole idea behind this trump-up."

Voight reddened. "You get balky with me and I'll snap my handcuffs on you."

"You mean, you'll try," Gresham said, emerging from the deep shadows to confront Deputy Voight. Now, up close in the open, it was possible to see the injuries he'd sustained. From hairline to jaw-hinge his flesh was crushed and battered until it was doubtful if he would ever heal without disfigurement. His purpled, puffed bruises and cuts were smeared with some sort of yellow salve concocted by Toledo, which was riveting from the rain down his seamed throat.

Stunned, Voight croaked out, "Judas Priest! Who beat you?"

"Guess."

Voight licked his lips and shuffled the papers.

"You don't need to guess. You know," Jessie said gently. "And you're not going to arrest him or anyone here, now or ever, for such nonsense."

"I got no trouble with you, Miz Starbuck," Voight said. "But the law is the law, and I'm not judge or jury, just a hit-and-miss wage-earner, and you damn well know that. I don't see where you think I'd do otherwise than serve these warrants."

"Have you a conscience?" she asked him.

"I have indeed; a very active one."

"And on what ground does your conscience stand?"

"It stands on decency. In essence, I suspect, it is very little different from yours."

"That's why you won't arrest anyone."

There was a moment of heavy, utter silence.

"I hate to pry," Deputy Voight said, stuffing the papers back in his pocket, "but would you mind telling me, Ki, why you had me summoned up here?"

Ki grinned. "Better than that, I'll show you."

Southward through the drizzle they rode, toward the loom of broken hills. With unerring instinct, Ki sought out the mouth of the cave, but passed it without comment and led them to the box end of the narrow canyon.

"We'll picket our mounts in the brush here, out of sight."

They made their horses comfortable and then stole back the few hundred yards to the cave mouth. Inside, nothing had been disturbed since Ki's last visit, and reckoning this was an instance where seeing was believing, Ki risked the few minutes required to unearth the gold and the body. Hurriedly covering them over again, Ki took Jessie and the fired-up Anvil men outside and told them:

"I don't know if anything will be happening. If anything does, my hunch is one or two guys will come with a wagon to haul off their loot. Don't stop them from going in. We have to catch them digging the stuff up, or they can weasel out of it with only a trespassing charge. Of course, if Voight and I don't stop them in there, you get them when they leave."

"What if we get other callers?" Finch asked.

"You stop them. The way you do it depends on the caller."

Jessie would have preferred to hide in the cave with Ki and Deputy Voight, but there simply wasn't the space. She joined Long Tom and his hands as they arranged themselves in a loose gantlet, hiding back far enough in the thickets alongside the canyon walls to be shielded.

Inside the cave, in a niche just beyond the grave and the gold-cache, Ki and Voight took their stand.

Slowly the hours passed, and Ki began to wonder if his hunch about the first rainy night might be pure hogwash. It was well past midnight when there was a sound in the direction of the cave mouth. Voices speaking in conversational tones reached them.

Voight nudged Ki, flashing a grin, and crouched low.

A light winked down the passage, drew steadily

nearer. By the blaze of a torch, Ki could see three figures approaching, two of them with shovels. Impatiently he waited while the shovels cleared dirt from the gold-cache.

"Hasn't been touched," a voice exulted. "It's all ours."

That was signal enough for Ki and Voight. They were stepping out of the niche when, totally unexpectedly, one of the figures drew his revolver and shot the man in front of him in the back. The victim was flung forward into the hole they'd dug, and above the deafening blast, his murderer was heard to sneer:

"Wrong! It's all mine!"

There was the scratch of a match, then a roaring flame shooting to the roof of the cave as the oiled waste caught fire. The whole scene was bright as day. Bathed in the radiance, dazzled by the unexpected glare, Curly Bub Becasse stood frozen, smoking revolver in hand. Behind him was the tall Katepwa brave, Shukka, holding a shovel, with another long-bladed butcher knife in his leggings. Sprawled ungainly in pooling blood was the banker, Thaddeus Ingersoll.

Revolver out and aimed, Voight bellowed: "You're arrested! Elevate!"

But the teamster and his assistant did not obey the order. The revolver in Becasse's hand was at full cock, his mind was set hair-trigger for kill, and he merely had to flick his gun hand level to shoot Voight point-blank. It was that infinitesimal fraction of time in which he flicked his gun hand level that wiped Becasse out. Even then, the two men fired nearly at the same time.

Becasse slammed around from Voight's slug, crashed into the side of the cave, and went down dead, his legs and arms tangled.

Death suddenly made his clothes seem too large for him.

The two shots, Voight's and Becasse's, roared out almost as one, and their reverberations had hardly pounded Ki's eardrums when Shukka came leaping, swinging the shovel. "Look out!" Ki yelled, diving at the Indian.

Too late. Voight was struck down with a terrible blow to the head. Ki ducked under Shukka's clubbing shovel and closed, grabbing at Shukka's corded wrist. A wrench and a twist and Shukka dropped his shovel with a howl of pain. But at the same instant, his right hand darted to his leggings and lashed up with his butcher knife, his lips peeled back and murder in his eyes.

Frantically Ki backpedaled for room to maneuver, narrowly missing being gutted as Shukka lunged after him. From a sheath at the waistband of his trousers, he whipped out his *tanto*, a short, delicately curved knife, single-edged and razor-sharp. Again Shukka leaped in with a slashing stroke. Ki moved his great body like a cat.

The Indian went past him, spinning before he came down on the balls of his feet. Ki laughed at him and they circled. Then Ki feinted three times, jerking his body to each side and forward. The Indian's body followed Ki's movements and then slashed out. Ki twisted sharply to one side. As Shukka's swipe cut thin air, Ki's knife flashed across to the Indian's knife-arm.

The blade came down across Shukka's upper arm

and laid it open to the bone. The knife dropped from his hand and he went to one knee. Ki stepped back and laughed. The Indian grunted with hatred and picked up his knife with his left hand. Ki let him come to his feet, then kicked out swiftly, cracking Shukka's wrist. The knife fell away from him and Ki stepped in, bringing his *tanto* down with a chopping motion across the biceps of Shukka's left arm. The Indian took the blow without a sound. His legs quivered once and his arms dangled uselessly, blood spurting with a gush.

Ki dropped his arm, reversing his hold on the hasp of the knife and coming up with it again almost in one long doubling motion. The blade struck home in the soft underbelly of the Indian. He collapsed against Ki. Ki laid his forearm across Shukka's breastbone and pushed hard, gripping his knife. Shukka's body spread-eagled backwards and crumpled to the ground where it lay unmoving. Ki quickly wiped his *tanto* blade clean on Shukka's shirt and slid it back in the sheath, then knelt beside the deputy.

Voight was already groaning with returning consciousness, and in a moment he sat up, rubbing his sore head. "This new hat saved me a busted skull," he mumbled. "She's thick and stiff."

They turned their attention to Thaddeus Ingersoll, then. The banker was still alive, but barely, and sinking fast. He glared into their faces with eyes of hate, raising himself with a last surge of strength and half fumbling, half patting the saddlebags on which he rested.

"Gold, you bastards," he panted. "Too—much—gold!"

With that lovely and magic and terrible word on his lips, he died.

Ki and Voight rose, but before either could say anything, from outside came a startled yelp, then a volley of gunfire. They raced to the mouth of the cave, where they saw the long sweep of guns blazing from the walls of the canyon. The Anvil riders poured a deadly barrage down on a wild mob of horsemen who were caught on the canyon floor. With shouts of shock and pain, the horsemen recoiled in wild pandemonium, managing to rally in a frantic effort to break out of this line of death.

The pathway and shouldering thickets became an inferno of pounding hoofs, rearing horses, roaring guns. As Ki and Voight joined the fray, it became a close-quarters melee of pistols and knives and hand-to-hand struggle with neither conscience nor mercy. Suddenly the shooting abated. Empty-saddled horses fishtailed skittishly amid the sprawl of corpses. Anvil men crowded around, whooping and laughing in the flush of victory, some converging on Ki to congratulate him on his hunch.

Ki smiled wanly. "It would've been nice to have a live one to talk to."

"You said stop them according to the callers, and they come calling with lead," Hughes said, "so we stopped them accordingly. Did we do right?"

"Yes."

"Y'know," Voight said thoughtfully, peering around at the bodies, "I don't recognize any of these critters offhand, but I betcha I'll find their descriptions in my stack of old wanted bulletins."

Indeed, the lean-bodied, hard-faced dead men had all been cut from the same mold. A certain coyote-like toughness about them tabbed them as renegades either up from the gold fields or in from the wild Northwest woods.

Finch spoke up, "Wal, a couple of their horses bear the Block-P brand."

"That seals it," Jessie said. "I was pretty sure there must be a tie-in between Pierce and his father-in-law, and this proves it. It also shows something else."

"Yeah, that not only was Curly Bub Becasse double-crossing Ingersoll," Ki said, "but that Ingersoll had plans to double-cross Becasse."

"Too much gold," Voight said. "Ingersoll never spoke righter."

"That, also," Jessie said, "but something more. It means Pierce has already gotten a new supply of gunmen."

Long Tom Hughes looked sick. "I think maybe we best be heading home."

"We're all riding over to the Anvil," Voight stated, "just as soon as we wrap up matters here."

"That'll take a while, and there're three M-Over-Y crewhands here who could probably handle the necessities," Ki suggested. Then, seeing Voight's dubious expression, he added, "If this were a twenty-dollar gold piece, we might have cause for concern, but this is truly too much gold for them to savvy. Especially gold with the notorious, thief-slaying Lochinvar Curse."

"The Lochinvar Curse? I never heard of no..." Voight paused, then chuckled craftily. "It has been effective, ain't it? I like it, I like it!"

Moments later, the eight were riding for the M-Over-Y ranch house. Setting as fast a pace as the darkness and rugged terrain would allow, Ki led the way with Jessie and Voight flanking him, the deputy persistent as a leech in drawing answers from him.

"Some of this is speculation," Ki admitted. "But we know Ingersoll learned about the gold somehow, and I kind of doubt the four bandits offered the information. Probably he came upon them right when he could see what they were packing. It was more than he could resist, and in another sense, they may not have given him any other choice."

"How d'you mean?"

"Well, chances are the bandits stopped at McQuade's for food, shelter, a rest, that sort of thing. Ingersoll blundered upon them, and kept from being killed immediately by fobbing himself off as the owner. They'd have killed the owner too, but after he'd supplied them food and drink. Or maybe he didn't feel threatened, and put on the act in order to get hold of the gold."

"But what was Ingersoll doin' there that night, and where was McQuade?"

"Ingersoll went to the M-Over-Y to see about the money McQuade owed him," Ki explained. "McQuade wasn't home, and probably didn't get back till the killing was over. Ingersoll didn't kill McQuade, though; Shukka did, while the old man was putting his horse in the stable."

"I can believe that Indian was along," Voight allowed. "Ingersoll went out collecting plenty of times with Shukka as his bodyguard."

"As his trouble-making thug," Jessie added. "Once you include Shukka, you involve Curly Bub Becasse, of course. Check the misfortunes that've happened to help the bank, and I imagine Becasse and his wagon will've been seen around at those times. But he's supposed to be out and about, that's his job, nothing unusual about it. Becasse wouldn't be suspected, and Pierce wouldn't be brought in except in extreme cases, there by leaving him innocent."

"Maybe so, Miss Jessie, maybe so. But let's stick to one can of worms at a time, for my sake. Ki, how do you know McQuade died stabling his horse?"

"By the feed boxes in the stalls. Recollect, Voight, I showed you five recently used feed boxes on one side of the stable? I didn't show you the two on the other side. One where Shukka's horse ate, and one with feed in it that hadn't been touched. I knew there had been six men in that kitchen, and that puzzled me for awhile, as only five men drank at the table. Shukka didn't drink with the others."

"Why?"

"Because he wouldn't have been able to take it."

"The poison?"

Ki smiled and shook his head. "No, not the poison. That was the point that had me fooled. To say that one man can slip poison into the glasses of four other men and keep his own clean at the same time is loco talk. It can't be done. But to slip something into the jug everybody is drinking from is easy, and that's just what Ingersoll did."

"Then why didn't it kill Ingersoll, too?"

"Because when Ingersoll was drinking with the other four, there wasn't any poison in the jug."

Baffled, Voight looked at Jessie. "Do you catch what he's saying?"

"It took us a bit to work it out last night," she admitted with a laugh. "Remember the second time

148

we talked with Doc Lozier in his office? He was just sending Ingersoll a packet of sleeping powder, and Doc remarked that Ingersoll used enough every night to put a horse to sleep. That's the trick. What Ingersoll did was slip a whopping amount of his sleeping powder into the jug, knowing he could withstand a dose that would knock the other men cold. When they began to pass out, he slipped in the poison and of course didn't take the last drink with them. They were too sleepy to notice that he didn't. That's why Shukka didn't drink at the table with them. The sleeping powder would've knocked him out, too. And of course the powder explains why they didn't have convulsions from the poison."

Ki went on, "Shukka's presence was important for another reason. It's mighty odd for anyone to carry poison around with them in quantity enough to drop four men. But it was natural for Ingersoll to carry sleeping powder. Well, as soon as we saw Shukka, Jessie spotted him for a Katepwa."

"The Katepwa are almost extinct now," Jessie told Voight. "But back when the Algonquin-speaking Indian tribes dominated the northwestern plains to the Rocky Mountains, the Katepwa was a mixed-blood border tribe between the Algonquin stock and the rival Shoshone group. As such, they were spurned by both sides yet dealt with both, and each sought them out to sabotage the other. Not surprisingly, poison became a specialty. A Katepwa can go out on a hillside and get together stuff in no time that'll cash in a roundup. They carry the stuff, too. So when Doc Lozier figured the four robbers died of an Indian poison, we naturally thought of Shukka."

"None of them knew what we were doing here,

but they didn't like it," Ki said. "Least of all Ingersoll, after Latigo Doyle remembered us from a time before. He bribed the telegraph operator, and when he figured we were snooping around he arranged for those men to ambush us in the alley."

"Still no sign of that third gent, and I expect he's long vamoosed," Voight said. "Say, didn't you suspect Yokum McQuade at any time?"

"Yes," Ki replied, "at first, because of the shoe marks under the table. They looked like marks made by house slippers. McQuade's cook and wrangler had been gone several days and the floor hadn't been swept. Dust was thick under there, and the prints were plain. But when I got a look at Ingersoll's congress gaiters, I saw they were shaped and heeled like house slippers, and that helped to tie him up with the business. And I've never known a truly respectable banker to tote a hideway gun. Oh, maybe a pocket piece at times, but never wearing a shoulder-holster rig."

Voight drew a deep breath. "I'm sure glad poor Yokum's name is clean."

"It looked bad for McQuade, all right," Ki said, nodding. "The bandits' four horses loaded with gold had vanished and McQuade and his horse with them. Ingersoll and Shukka had to use the horses to pack the gold and McQuade's body, and after they'd salted everything away, they took the horses off with them, all but the lame one I backtracked to the cave. Anyway, their next step was to arrange with Becasse to have him sneak it out of this section in the course of his freighting business. Miss Wyndam, happening along unexpectedly, complicated things for them, and made them hustle to get the gold out. Otherwise,

150

Ingersoll would've taken over the ranch and they could've taken their time."

About then the M-Over-Y ranch house came into view, and they spurred forward into the yard. Beth Wyndam and the crew came out to greet them.

The get-together was short and not very sweet. Deputy Voight, faltering with hat in hand, managed to inform Beth that Yocum McQuade had been discovered dead. Beth had resigned herself to the loss of her uncle; she knew without being told that a vanishment like his most always entailed tragedy. With a face set like stone, and silent tears riveting down her cheeks, she continued to carry out what she felt were her "obligations," grieving with a certain stoic resolve that impressed everyone, especially Long Tom Hughes.

"Brave gal," Hughes later told Ki. "She sure can take a big blow."

To which Ki agreed, noting she gave as good as she got. However, at the moment his concern was giving directions to the cave so the M-Over-Y crew could recover McQuade's remains, which they were to wagon in with the other bodies to Dr. Lozier, after they cached the sachels here. Voight conjured up a legend to embellish the Lochinvar Curse, warning the curse applied to gossips and rumor-mongers as well as gold robbers. By their pop-eyed expressions, Ki doubted the three, even Latigo, would peep a word, much less grab the gold.

Beth was puzzled by much of this, of course, but lengthy explanations had to wait, and besides, she was too busy to listen. She had kept her big dinner warming for Ki's return, and made the mistake of mentioning food within earshot of the Anvil crew.

They demolished the dinner in nothing flat. She raced about, trying to keep pace while there was a speck left to serve...and everywhere that Beth went, Hughes' sheep-eyes were sure to go.

As they left, the first stray handful of heavy rain fell in great drops, like skinned grapes. When it stopped, it seemed finished, exhausted Deputy Voight was not through questioning, however, and for the first part of their ride to the Anvil, he badgered Jessie and Long Tom Hughes to spill the beans. But they steadfastly refused, insisting Rawhide was foaming at the mouth for the chance to enlighten the deputy.

Then, in a golden lacework of lightning, the cloudburst came, with a howling gale. It came with a thunderclap like a blow from a gigantic mallet that smote the eardrums to deafness, and with an aftereffect that seemed to continue to pound into them, with padded, soundless raps. The rain rode in then, on the wind, with a force and volume that seemed to tilt the ebony world.

For what seemed like hours they fought the fury; then, gradually, the wind dropped. In time, the rain ceased as well. The overcast cracked, split, and drifted like an ice flow; and a blue, moonlit dome took shape above them.

When they rode in, the Anvil ranchstead seemed singularly quiet. Moonlight was bright in the yard, glazing the packed earth with a pattern of milky green and lavender blotched with jet black shadows, yet not a man showed as they rode up to the main house and Hughes called out.

Silence answered him.

"I'll ride round to the bunkhouse and ask the boys," Everett suggested.

They sat their horses in silence as Everett rode swiftly in the direction of the bunkhouse. After a moment they saw him returning, his face blank.

"There ain't nobody there," he said.

Hughes dismounted, saying, "I'm going in."

They all went in calling for Rawhide, for anybody. The silence that answered them was broken abruptly by a faint, scratching sound, coming from the direction of the parlor. Hughes whirled in that direction—to halt in the doorway with a strangled groan.

The scratching sound had been made by a woman who, humped over grotesquely, was crawling toward them along the floor. It was Bertha. As they stared aghast, she struggled to gasp out shrilly:

"Pierce . . . come, kill . . . take Mist' . . . Avalon . . . kill me . . ."

Farther along, between the parlor and the ranch-office, the figure of a man was slumped, face upward, teeth showing through his drooping, sandy mustache. Jessie winced, averted her face. The man's skull had been split open with a meat cleaver. The broad blade still buried in his brain.

"Bertha got one of 'em!" Hughes exclaimed, walking into the dining room, which had four windows facing toward the creek. Three men were sprawled out here, and against the wall, and facing the window was a fourth who, as they approached, addressed them in a husky whisper. It was Toledo, who'd stayed at the Anvil to doctor the others.

"They done come here two, three hours ago . . . Pierce an' p'raps a dozen others. . . . We see 'em

153

coming an' holed up in here. . . ." His head fell forward; he lifted it, after a long moment, with a faint grin. "They done plugged yours truly at the first go-off; they got me, but that's okay. . . . We got a number of 'em in exchange, an' Bertha split the noggin on one of 'em. . . . When you meet up with that bugger, remem—member us. . . ."

★

Chapter 11

It was a somberly determined group that rode out from the Anvil. They had departed after laying out and covering those who had died with their boots on, and now were following a warm trail left by the raiders. There was no particular mystery as to where it led, nor had there been any attempt to hide the tracks; so they were able to pursue at a rapid trot, northeasterly in the direction of the Block-P.

Back at the ranch, Jessie and Hughes had told Deputy Voight what he would have heard from Rawhide. They gave a concise, albeit edited, version of events since his last visit and ending with last night's raid. It still left the puzzle of the corpses in Doc Lozier's office, but now as they rode along that was not the problem bothering Voight. He might've asked Hughes about it, but Hughes was up front keeping track with Ki, and in no humor to chat, his eyes merely blazing points. Voight sidled in alongside Jessie, smiled, and said:

"Just one question more. A personal one. Do you actually believe that any one man—Pierce, for instance—could whip the whole county into cowtowing? Do you believe he'd rule Anvil, and Lazy R, and every other ranch from one end of the valley to the other?"

"Yes. Pierce and Ingersoll at the bank could've whipsawed control of one ranch after another," Jessie answered. "I can't say they would have, if that was their motive. But I believe there was more than that behind their wanting the Anvil."

"Really? What?"

"Rustling. As a depot for stolen herds traveling the Lechuza Trail, for instance, or as a holding pen for local, small-time thefts, such as you said the Furrow cousins were wont to pull. To make it practical, though, Pierce needs a path connecting the Block-P and the Lechuza. And the only path anywhere close around is smack through Anvil land."

"Why, so it is, so it is. . . ."

Hughes called out, pointing out the landmark, the crest with its double chimneys and arch of stone. The Block-P lay in that direction, at the far end of a basin, on a squat, rimrock butte like a battlement. From this vantage, riflemen could have ambushed the Anvil riders, but the group sped headlong into the trap—if it was a trap—with reckless disregard.

Ki, glancing at Hughes at his elbow, saw the foreman's grim face per questioningly at the heights ahead. Following Hughes's gaze, he perceived a figure high up on the rim—the figure of a horse and rider. It vanished even as he looked, but just for a

156

heartbeat, it seemed to him that he'd glimpsed others against the moonlit sky.

They swung up toward the Block-P ranch on its wagon trail, some miles still between them and the compact circle of buildings. Hughes, unslinging his binoculars, centered them not upon the ranch, but upon the place where the figure had appeared. Abruptly he cursed and wrenched the reins hard right, forcing his horse to swerve off trail. Close behind veered the others.

"Get down!" he shouted to the riders, but with his warning, the air cracked with the rush of bullets. The slugs were not coming from behind or directly ahead along the trail, but from that rim.

Dismounting and taking cover in the chaparral, the Anvil crewmen unlimbered their saddle carbines and began returning fire. Finch had been wounded in the first salvo, but not badly; the bullets, most of them, kept going a good two feet over their heads. Jessie, zeroing in on the rimrock just below the spot where the figure had been seen, levered round after round upward in a steady stream.

There came a faint yell as a man, leaping to full height, was outlined for a moment against the night. In a tenth of a second he became a target for the Anvil crew, and at the impact of their bullets, he staggered and toppled. For a moment he hung, head downward, and a hand reached clawing at his ankles; then, limp as a bag, he slid down the long, steep slope and landed very near the brush where the Anvil crew was crouching.

The dead man was dressed as a puncher in chaps and faded shirt. Yet it was the sight of his face, mahogany-colored, which made Hughes exclaim: "Injun! A Modoc buck!"

That would account for the poor aim, even with unsuspecting targets in plain view. Modocs were notoriously bad marskmen; it was the thing that, in the Modoc War, had given the troopers an edge. Everett added, "Reckon him and a few buddies have strayed off'n the compound. Maybe somebody might've, ah . . . financed them, eh?"

Jessie was pretty certain that Everett had voiced the truth. Pierce had hired the buck and his companions to hinder the pursuers' advance. A few scattering shots came from the rimrock; then, outlined against the moonlight they saw horsemen, but before they could fire at them, they were gone.

In all, the Anvil force had been held up not more than a quarter of an hour. But time counted heavily. If Pierce was still on the short-handed side, as he probably was, the element of time would work in his favor. All the Anvil men were sure that he'd kidnapped Rawhide for one purpose, to extort the ranch from him one way or another, and thereby squelch any complaints about raiding and murder against him. And they were equally convinced that Pierce contemplated violence, most likely death, to Rawhide when all was said and done.

Continuing on, they rode for the ranch now at a swift pace. When the Block-P buildings came into sight, the riders thinned out, then charged, yelling. They were met with silence, and an air of emptiness about the place like there'd been about the Anvil ranchstead.

The horse corrals were empty save for a few glue-foot nags, which stood idly switching their tails.

From the cookshack arose a spiral of smoke, though, and Jessie found herself wondering how long ago the Block-P had skedaddled en masse. She rode around the shack, pistol out, her keen gaze boring into the shadows, for the thought also occurred to her that the Block-P had not left, but had set up another trap.

No one seemed to be there, however. Then, as she rode from behind an angle of the bunkhouse, she heard a sudden gunshot. It was followed by faint, feeble swearing. Quickening, Jessie rounded the corner and saw three men sitting in the moonlight, cursing Finch and Gresham, who were covering them with drawn weapons.

One of the trio was hooting sarcastically, "Wal, if here don't come the big killers. Say, if'n I was half a man, which the same I ain't only a quarter, I'd have plugged you guys first—eh, only joking, Dep'ty Voight."

Voight grunted disgustedly as he stalked forward, frowning at the trio. The bigmouth had his arm in a sling. The other two looked as if they'd been run over by a stampede, and plainly all three were on the Block-P's invalid list, recovering from wounds. They scowled, heads down, muttering curses.

With Anvil and the law in temporary possession of Pierce's ranch, Jessie and Ki and Deputy Voight wanted to do a little investigating around. They knew the need for hurry, yet were unable to pass up a golden opportunity.

"Besides," Voight told Jessie, "we might find something that'll speed our search."

They and the Anvil crew fanned out around the yard and buildings. Voight, who'd read up on Overlooked Hiding Places of Hunted Criminals, went to inspect the outhouses. Jessie headed for the farthest shed to check a hunch—although in one respect it was more than a hunch; it was common sense that'd become common practice: Keep explosives safely distant.

The shed door had a padlock, but as if left in haste, the lock was hanging open. Inside, Jessie found a meager store of blasting supplies. There were a few caps and coils of double-tape fuse, a rusted fuse cutter and crimper, and the dregs of a keg of shotgun black powder. Shelved apart were boxes of wads, shot, and similar odds and ends, along with a fair heap of trash. Nothing she was looking to find.

Jessie was about to pack up her hunch and leave, when she glimpsed a wooden case in the trash under the workbench. It was empty, the top gone, but on the side of the case was the name of a feed firm. That put it enough out of place her for her to drag the case out for a study. On one end was tacked a ripped shipping label showing the first three letters of the consignee's name: P-I-E-. The rest was torn off. Both sides had the feed firm name, looking to be fresh stencils, and seem to cover some other name underneath.

She took the case outside and scrutinized it in the moonlight. After a moment, she spotted Deputy Voight and called to him, beckoning him over. She wasn't sure he heard her, though, for he was bounding and flinging about the yard, making all sorts of wild noises while swatting the air and himself with his hat, as though he were performing some lunatic Mexican fandango. He lurched out of sight around the barn, but a few moments later he walked calmly over to Jessie, or as calmly as he could while panting and wheezing for breath.

160

"You call me?"

"Yes. I ran across something."

"So did I."

"Oh, was that it? You were celebrating?"

Voight shook his head. "Mud-dauber wasps' nest under a seat."

Jessie showed him the box and told him to look closely. "You can make out most of another company's name under the bold stenciling."

"Uh-huh. E. I. du Pont de Nemours and Company. The powder makers."

"You're holding the answer to how Pierce made the blame fall on Rawhide," Jessie said. "Rawhide ordered a case of powder legitimately. It's a costly hassle, having to be freighted in by regular powder trains at double first-class rate. From the Grant's Pass depot, how must it've gone to Rawhide?"

"By Curly Bub Becasse."

"Right. And this powder must've come the same way, wherever Pierce may've bought it, even by mail order. The guys on the powder train wouldn't have disguised this box, so it has to've been Becasse in direct cahoots with Pierce, smuggling powder in canisters resembling Rawhide's cans. Whenever Block-P raiders blew stuff up, it appeared only Anvil could be to blame; and due to the spy, Sumpter, stealing from Rawhide's supply, Rawhide had unexplainable losses that made him seem guiltier. Meantime, the Block-P powder remained a secret."

"And likely Pierce took what was left," Voight said worriedly.

Suddenly a loud shouting match erupted up by the main house. Jessie and Voight, tossing the case inside the shed, sprinted off in that direction.

Meanwhile Ki went through the main house, which appeared deserted. He marveled at the elaborate layout, the costly furniture and oriental rugs, as he methodically searched each room, each nook and cranny. He was not quite finished when he too heard the noisy row coming from outside. It rose to a yelling crescendo, then abruptly peaked with two hammering crunches, and driveled off into groans and whimpers. Ki took the easiest way and vaulted out an open window, and found Long Tom Hughes herding two men before him at gunpoint, and Jessie and Voight hurrying up from beyond the barn.

Seeing them, Hughes called out with a laugh: "This here is Jinglebob Ashburton and t'other is Ed Pucheim. Ain't they a fine pair to draw to? I found 'em living the good life, and that's the truth, hiding in the hay loft with plenty of booze and cigars."

The two swarthy, tough-looking young men, in their mid-twenties, maybe, were stumbling forward, wincing, rubbing their heads and moaning. Jinglebob Ashburton wore mustard yellow chaps, tight, legging style. Ed Pucheim was noticeable for his stiff leather cuffs, almost elbow-length, decorated in nailhead brads. Ki wouldn't have liked either one of them near any stray cash of his, lying, say, on a bartop.

In that deceptively mild tone of his, Deputy Voight said to them, "You gents are supposed to be dead, don't you know. Blown up, sky-high."

Pucheim started, "Warn't our idea—ouch!"

Ashburton had kicked him. "You can't prove nuthin', lawman. Braining us with a pistol butt won't get us to talk, either."

"I don't plan to try. I plan to put you in Cell Three and watch over you," Voight said, his face growing

162

red and seeming to expand. "Here I'm getting along nice and quiet with a few drunk and disorderlies, and a few disturbings of the peace, and a few chicken stealings, and now this. I've been in law for over twenty years, and this is going to be my worst winter."

"We'll make it so," Ashburton sneered.

"In a way, you will. Word will spread to the ranchers who've been robbed by my Block-P prisoners. And these same ranchers will go get together with a few of their friends and make the ride to Unity, even if the snow is withers deep. And when they get here, you know what they'll want to do?"

"What?" Pucheim asked, sweating.

"They'll want to borrow whoever's on tap here, like you and Mist' Ashburton, just for a little while, just for an afternoon trip out around to see the sights. Naturally I can't lend you, and there'll be vilification and bad lingo, and maybe even deeds."

"I'm a state's witness," Pucheim quavered, "I'm going to testify for the persecution."

"Naw, I am," Ashburton declared, "I know more dirty shit than Ed."

"Is that so?" Voight said, interested. "Of course, I can't offer no threats, nor inducements, nor enticements, or anything like 'em, but I'm sure the prosecutor will be happy to hear that's how your inclinations run. Well, let's hear."

Jessie's eyes gleamed as she listened to the two men battling to confess. The matter was simple: they were, along with the riderless horses, part of a plot to discredit Rawhide. They were to remain out of sight afterwards, and Pierce would probably have made

163

sure they did, permanently, if events hadn't caught up with everyone so fast and furiously.

Lately Pierce had not done too well—ever since, he was convinced, that crazy gunbitch shot Kuttner and the Kid by some contrary fluke of nature. His sneak attack night before last had failed, with a dead Block-P'er left behind as evidence. Guntraps were rigged that night and in town the next day, to stop Anvil from reaching Voight, and Voight was tricked out of town with the horse thieving stunt. It worked; they retrieved the body, plus an extra. And Pierce had it wide open to make his big move last night, an all-out assault to destroy the Anvil which ended in disaster. And those two bodies wound up swiped, to boot.

But Pierce had his bad luck turn good today, when he was able to abduct Rawhide. Naturally the Anvil crew would hit his Block-P ranch right off, so naturally Pierce vamoosed from here with all his able-bodied gunmen. Pierce, ironically, had to keep Rawhide safe from danger as well as rescue, until he'd succeeded in extorting what he wanted. So, in a sense, it didn't matter if Ashburton and Pucheim, along with the three wounded gunmen, were left behind and found. Even though they were living proof of his treachery, Pierce was counting on the fact that the Anvil crew couldn't do much of anything for fear of harming Rawhide. And if the Anvil crew went to the law, it wouldn't do them much good, for his deal with Rawhide would include smoothing over the fight.

However, the one detail Pierce had ignored in his haste and arrogance was that among those he ditched behind might be somebody who'd know where he took Rawhide. Another fine point he'd overlooked was that Deputy Voight might conceivably show up, here or at the Anvil, before the stage could be set to bamboozle him further.

"We'll take this pair o' devils along with us and . . ." Hughes trailed off, scowling to emphasize his unspoken threat.

Pucheim and Ashbruton piped up in unison: "South! Southeastward to big Blue Mountain!" they chorused.

Jessie figured it was likely the truth, considering they agreed. At least it was a lead. There was now no reason for another moment's delay. Pierce by now had gotten off to a long head start, a start which would be difficult to overcome. And, following a cold trail, it would be like looking for the proverbial needle to try and locate him in the wilderness of chasms and crests that comprised 5800-foot-high Blue Mountain. Still, with the information given by these two, they had a chance. Being their only chance, they took it.

They struck out southeasterly at a fast pace, with Ashburton and Pucheim at the head of the parade, faces glum and hapless. If Anvil didn't string 'em up, then Pierce would shoot out their lights.

The miles flowed steadily by, their unflagging persistence taking a toll of their mounts, but paying off in making up time over distance. The nearer they drew to Blue Mountain, the more disordered appeared the terrain. By the time they reached the broken foothills, the escarpments were a forbidding chaos of angles, planes, strata, and cleavages. It was as if nature had set out to erect a magnificent edifice, then had wearied and abandoned it midway through.

Eventually they came to the lower lip of the foothills, and stopped by the eroded bank of a centuries-dry riverbed. It made a rubble-strewn hairpin bend at this point, forming what was, in effect, two trails wending back into the broad rise of hills. Either one was suitable for Pierce's purposes.

Voight glanced at Pucheim. "Which way?"

Pucheim shrugged, looking hopefully at Ashburton. Ashburton shook his head. "Listen, honest, from here we dunno which way to go."

Dismounting, they started scouting around the old river bed. Unruh was the first to find numerous tracks plunging down in the thick, muddy bottom of a large rainpuddle. "The left is where some riders went not long ago," he said.

Ki concurred and, remounting, scanned the striated battlements ahead. "We'll be hard to miss, riding by," he remarked to Jessie.

"Well, if Pierce has gunmen waiting for us," she replied, sighing, "our waiting around out here isn't going to help it any."

They pushed on, snaking across the raw, seared foothills through the gorge formed by the riverbed. Soon it led to a maze of connecting gulches and culverts. Once above the first low set of foothills, more squashed prints in soggy ground led them into ever-steepening rimrocks and winding, boulder-strewn ravines. Most often they just saw stone, ranging from pebbles to vast fissured slabs, and shadow where the moonlight failed to penetrate. But increasingly, as they wound higher, they noticed juniper patches contrasting their darker pattern against the common sagebrush and thatches of bluebunch grass, and scraggly, windswept conifers clinging to ledges and clefted slopes.

Unceasingly, Ki surveyed their bleak terrain, even while trying to keep a mental map of their convoluted course. Each gap, fringe, and thicket was a potential menace. Each tall crag and beetling spire was a possible watchtower for ruthless eyes. Even the placid moonlit calm within these enclosing elevations was a hushed yet vibrant warning to his suspicious ears.

It turned out, to their intense relief, to be a false alarm. At an exclamation from Long Tom Hughes, they all checked their horses at a small, fast-rilling stream that ran crosswise to the trail. The horses had smelled the water, and thirstily lapped from the flowing trickle as the riders dismounted to stretch their legs.

It was then that the riders heard, faintly yet unmistakably, the murmur of voices and the sound of hoofbeats upon stone. Deputy Voight raised his hand for silence, his face wearing a perplexed expression. Ki, too, felt puzzled. Evidently they had stumbled upon the rear-guard of Pierce's guncrew, and if they hadn't been halted by the stream, they may well have smacked right into them in the darkness.

Jessie leaned close to Ki and whispered, "We made pretty good time, considering. But I didn't think we'd gotten *this* close to them."

They eased forward, slowly now. They might have gambled on stampeding Block-P gunmen by a sudden, swift charge, but there was Rawhide to be considered. So there was little to be done other than to trail along, with the chances of being discovered increasing with every passing moment.

167

The moon was on the wane, and dawn was yet some hours away. The night wind, which had been blowing in their direction, now shifted so that the sounds in front of them died away. They seemed to move in a murky well of silence, their horses' breathing and light clicking of irons the loudest sounds of all.

They must be coming close. . . .

Ki was straining his gaze against the shadowy crevices, his ear attuned to the night noises. A feeling strengthened in him that somewhere, somehow, they'd made a mistake. Intuitively, he sensed an absence of something, of something missing, out of place. . . .

They had been going steadily upward. Then, abruptly, the ground dipped on a downward slant, and Ki was able to discern more of the trail ahead. He swore and called irritably to the deputy, "Rein in your posse, Voight. We've been fed a bum steer."

"You're right," Voight agreed, focusing on where Ki was pointing.

It was the thing that Ki had felt without being able to get a handle on, the thing that Jessie had nearly tumbled to when she'd expressed her doubt that they had come so close so fast. Roughly two hundred yards ahead of them rode three horsemen. They were moseying along as if they had nowhere to go and plenty of time to do it in, eyes front, reins slack, letting their mounts pick their going.

"Goddamn to high hell! Pierce sure sly-foxed us," Hughes growled irately, unlimbering his Sharps. "Well, I'll see if I can't whittle the odds."

"Don't fire!" Jessie cried urgently. "Put the rifle down, please."

168

"What? Why not?" he demanded, rankling. "You on their side?"

"We all feel like you do, Long Tom, but now *think*. You shoot, you hit one of them, at a risk of signaling our position, bogging us in a gunfight with the two you don't hit, and having them a rearguard threat the whole way back."

"You're right, Jessie; sorry," Hughes admitted, sheathing his Sharps. "It's Rawhide we want."

"And we won't get, at this rate," Ki remarked with a sour grin. "Those three were falling back, and when we were watering our horses, they were riding slow on purpose. Pierce and the bulk of his crew may have slipped down off the mountain and be long gone by now."

"I don't care, I'm going to find 'em. I'm going to trace Rawhide if I have to search every foot of ground 'twixt here and Argentina." Hughes faced Ki squarely, and his narrowed eyes held a desolate look. "If Pierce and his guncrew hurt Rawhide, God help 'em, 'cause I'll kill every last one with my bare hands!"

★

Chapter 12

Wheeling his horse, Hughes called to his crew, "This here's a blind trail, boys. Turn back! Pierce, he didn't figure maybe to be tailed so closely, but he played it safe."

After riding back to the meager stream, everyone started the arduous, time-consuming chore of checking their twisting backtrail. Carefully they surveyed the nearly inscrutable rubbled path and numerous animal tracks, looking for any mud-sunken tracks made in the last rainstorm, their task complicated by the lack of light and the hoofprints of their own horses when they'd first come this way.

Eventually, after following their meandering course back through the rough wilderness, Gresham let out a whoop. He motioned toward a narrow gap, hardly more than a black slit in the surrounding rock

171

slopes, and proudly announced, "Through there, see? Boys, they filed through there."

Ki and Voight rode into the gap which, once past the initial slim entrance, widened out enough to qualify as another canyon. The ground here was obliterated by a churning mass of hoofmarks, lumps of fresh dung, and the wet soakings of urine. They moved forward a short distance, leaning over in their saddles for closer scrutiny, and it quickly became apparent that a small band had stopped here to gather, mounted on shod horses.

Calling the others in to join them, Ki and Voight headed the way along the canyon. It proved no better than the one they'd taken past the stream, twisting and writhing in sundry directions as if in primeval torment, and it behooved them to go slow, for anywhere along its course would make an excellent spot for ambush. But so far there had been no sign of a trap.

Presently they came upon a granite outcropping, around which the trail bent and doubled around a steep, mountainous slope, and then entered a small plateau. They halted, again casting about for sign.

Jessie, her glance on the scrub lining one edge of the plateau, leaped down from her horse. "Look at this!" she called, and held up a torn strip of white cloth caught on a branch. It was a small ripped section of gauze bandage, of the type Rawhide's wound had been bound with.

"Ain't that just like the boss, eh?" Hughes declared with a chuckle.

Following that course through some scrawny timber, they came upon a second small strip of bandage. They were on no false trail this time; Rawhide had been clever in using the bandage to help lead any rescuers across the plateau, and now all eyes were kept peeled for a third strip as they continued back in amongst the ridges and ravines.

Another mile, perhaps, went by, with the going getting steadily rougher, when the way finally grew too imposing for the tuckered horses. They dismounted and began leading their mounts, trudging for some distance until, with a muttered oath, Voight called a halt.

They were bone tired. It had been some time since they'd found the last sign from Rawhide, and caution as well as exhaustion counseled a wait till dawn. It was more than merely the menace of an ambush; the moon had now waned to the point where its frail glow was almost nonexistent, but the eastern horizon had yet to show the slightest indication of the coming day. The darkness was like a wolf's throat. They hadn't the foggiest notion where they were or where they were going, and had long since lost all ability to ferret out any tracks.

Ki rested a moment, then took an exploratory hike onward. He quickly found himself stepping off into nothing, and leaped backward with a startled oath. In the brief glimpse he'd had, he'd made out that this was the edge of a ravine, its steep walls dropping into a depthless black abyss below.

"Stay put," he warned, and retracing his steps, he bent down and quartered the surface like a hound. Abruptly he gave a soundless whistle. The trail, which had led them to this sudden ledge, cut off sharply from it to the right. Pierce, overlooking nothing, had once again deliberately misled them, counting on them riding—not walking—full-tilt to the point and over.

And then, with the hoofprints leading hard right along the ridge of the ravine, from the cliff-face there came a burst of bullets. The slugs whined among them with a buzzing as of angry bees.

With the first volley, Jinglebob Ashburton was shot dead and Finch was wounded, and one of the horses toppled slowly over with lead in its hind quarters. The gunfire was coming from high up, with the marksmen themselves invisible, and what with the rearing and plunging of the horses and the incessant hammerings of the hidden guns, the slender ridge was too much of a bedlam for anyone to draw a bead on the ambushers.

"Down! Get down!" Voight shouted, trying to restore some order. "Get your horses back out of the way! Move!"

They ran their horses for the shelter of the rimrock. Once their mounts were stowed out of sight, they scurried for cover while salvoes from the enemy above ravaged down around them. There was no way of retaliating save by an attack in force—and a frontal assault in either direction would leave them exposed to fire. It was some small compensation when a Block-P gunnie leaned far out to draw a bead on them. Jessie fired, almost without taking aim. They saw the man's hat fly off, with it a tuft of hair like a scalplock, as his body toppled into the ravine. Fact remained, they were stuck, hard pressed to find shelter, crouching among the scrub and boulders with no targets to shoot back at and no way of retreating or going forward.

Worriedly, Ki scanned the surrounding area. "I

174

wonder if one man could make it up and around," he thought aloud.

Voight, catching Ki's voiced notion, glanced at the rocky cliff-face and then at Ki, horrified. "Forget it," he barked. "It's suicide!"

But Ki was already sliding away from his concealing rocks. "Cover me."

"Don't be daft! Come back here!"

Ki merely shook his head and began climbing along the slope toward the next outcropping. There came sudden yells from above, and the rimrock roared with the reports of rifles, the high whine of slugs ending in a succession of thumps and shrill ricochets. Through the darkness grit spurted and shards of stone flew as Ki continued clawing desperately from one mound of rocks to another thin lip of a ledge.

A moment later, Ki slewed out of sight and apparently out of range of the Block-P sharpshooters. Yet, cautious as ever, he continued making his slow ascent toward the rimrock of the slope. Down below with the others, his odds were rotten; they got far worse as he progressed, and he soon found himself on a triangular ledge with no apparent way up or down other than the way he'd just climbed. Crosswise, however, were a few handholds upward along the craggy face of the abutment. And almost straight above the abutment rose stone like the walls of a tower to the crest.

Inching across, Ki climbed the abutment with relative ease. Scaling the sheer, pitted walls adjoining it, however, proved to be treacherous and exhausting. Finally easing over the top, he flattened prone, trying to catch his breath for that last desperate ascent, hearing the shale sliding in a trickle down the way he'd come.

Then he started forward, keeping low and in line with the ridge. Beneath him he could hear the exchange of gunfire, but it was more desultory now, fanning between times into sudden bursts.

Worming through a low hedge of scrub, Ki peered around. Above him loomed yet another cliff; far below was the edge of the ravine where the others were trapped. Directly below, much closer to him, was the thin line of what, he assumed, was one of the numerous slender ledges projecting from the eroded mountain slope. He couldn't see what or who was on the ledge, but he could hear the acrimony in the voices of two bitter enemies arguing below.

"You're a suck-egg hound, a disgrace to the lowest cur in the region, Felix Pierce. I'll ne'er be party to your foul abominations!"

"I'm giving you your last chance, Rawhide! You don't give, I'll plug you and give you down to your boys!" Pierce's laugh was caustic, malevolent. "And then I'll have my boys give yours up to the devil, y'hear?"

"Git about your murderin' business, then, why don't you? You're piss-ant yaller, is why, a sniveling leech, and you know it. Go to hell!"

Ki stiffened, searching for some way to intervene. Whatever he did, though, it couldn't be done from here. Hastily he headed along the ridge, hunting for a way down to the ledge where Pierce and Rawhide were squaring off. A few yards along, he found a spot—not good, but better than anywhere so far— and scrambled downward, tamping the sandlike gravel of the steep slope until it became sufficiently solid to bear his weight without landsliding noisily.

Descending to what, he reckoned, was the proper ledge, he now saw why Pierce had chosen it for his vantage point. From here he was concealed from those below, but could survey the Anvil men and Jessie herded together in the scant cover near the ravine. A bit below and to the left, most of the Block-P ambushers were situated in the rocks, keeping up a scattering fire practically without return. A little further along on his right, some half-dozen Block-P gun-thugs were nestled on a scarp, having outflanked the Anvil bunch, preventing them from escaping in that direction.

There was no doubt in Ki's mind that to save Rawhide, he'd have to act damn fast. Nor did he doubt that once he started something, Jessie and Hughes and the others would surge instantly into action. But he failed to see the face, with its bestial eyes and implacable, grim mouth . . . and he almost failed to catch the motion behind him along the ledge, where a Block-P gun-thug was swinging up his carbine, its muzzle aiming full at Ki's heart.

He heard the crunch of woody brush, and pivoting, snapped a *shuriken* winging toward the sound. A burly gunman reared, his left hand tossing aside his rifle and clawing at his throat, where the *shuriken* protruded from his blood-spurting larynx. His right arm was jerking, windmilling erratically, his hand keeping hold of some object with a deathlike grip. Ki couldn't make out what the man was clenching, other than it wasn't another firearm. Then the man was arcing over the edge of the ridge, plunging toward the scarp where some of the Block-P guncrew were collected.

At the fall of the man, yells echoed along the rockface. Ki could see the Block-P men scrambling away—and at the instant, something flashed past his face. Instinctively he put up a hand, snatching at it, then recoiling.

It was a canister of black powder, with fuse burning. Flung diagonally, it had come from the crest he'd just descended, indicating that way was no longer open for escape. Well, he'd be blown up there if he didn't get rid of this can, Ki thought frantically; and he hurled it where he felt it'd do the most good, down in the boulders where most of the Block-P men were mustered.

An instant later, the boulders cascaded bursting high into the night. What appeared to be chunks of timber were thrown up and out; they were not timber, but the broken bodies of men. Hard upon the first explosion, a second erupted down over by the scarp. Dazzled by the twin blasts, Ki realized that the object gripped by that one gunman must've been another powder can—one which the man had been rising up to toss at the Anvil forces below when he'd spotted Ki on the ledge. Now, instead, with deafening concussions, this and the first detonation were hurtling belching thick smoke and debris and human flesh down onto the Block-P's intended victims crouching by the ravine.

By the suddenly sprouting incandescence, Ki saw that the Block-P mob was staggered, shocked senseless if not downright stunned or killed. And together, Voight and Hughes were up and running, the Anvil crew charging with him, firing their weapons as they leaped up the rock-face, yelling encouragement to one another.

Ki also glimpsed, as he turned along the narrow ledge, a man with his chest and one arm wound in gauze bandage. It was Rawhide, and he was leaning far out over the edge. Behind him was Pierce, bracing himself against the cliff and forcing the Anvil owner outward, inch by inch. From that crumbling rim, the cliff plunged downward hundreds of feet in a sheer, sickening fall. Rawhide, almost spread-eagled against the rim, seemed from Ki's distance to be pinned there like a fly, on the verge of being pried loose and shoved over.

Ki tore into a run, his weapons impractical until he drew closer, and besides, Rawhide was between him and Pierce. But not for long. He'd be too late, he knew; he couldn't possibly close fast enough to save Rawhide.

Seemingly out of nowhere, then, a figure flashed down the rock-face to land catlike on feet and fingers, on the other side of the struggling ranchers. Startled, Ki watched Rawhide stumble, stretch outward . . . then beheld the trim figure, a woman's figure, dart in with drawn pistol to attack Pierce.

Jessie!

Pierce swiveled and made a swiping lunge at her. Jessie saw it coming and was ahead of him, triggering as she backed aside a pace. The heavy slug from her revolver struck, spinning Pierce halfway around. He'd been hit in the side, and whether it was a vital spot or not, the shocking power of that bullet staggered him.

Ki, anticipating Pierce would fall, sprinted for Rawhide.

But Pierce did not fall. A look flared in his eyes, a look made up of a mixture of fear, and desperation,

179

and crazed fury. The look of a man determined to leave this world in a slavering frenzy, anybody and everybody dying with him.

He charged Jessie. She was triggering another shot when he was upon her, swinging his arm, batting it away. Her gun was gone, thumping across the darkened ledge. He seized her by the wrist, dragged her forward, and for a moment she was against him, hard, then with feline quickness she twisted away.

He rushed her again. Eyes shifting and alert, Jessie bent double, dodged sideward. The quickness of it almost eluded Pierce, but his hand swung out, grabbed her left forearm. Her expected move now was to twist aside, perhaps go to the ground. Instead she moved close, and the impact of her body made him fall back half a step, almost scraping the edge with one heel. He rebounded, carrying her against the wall of the ledge, pinning her there and using his weight to overpower her.

Jessie was like a mountain cat, fighting him. Her teeth were bared, the fingernails of her left hand slashing his flesh like talons. Her right hand, finally working its way free of his crushing embrace, brought up the derringer she kept behind her belt buckle, which she had managed to grab unseen when she'd bent double and dodged forward. She raised the little two-barrel weapon now, jabbed the muzzle in his ear, and triggered.

Pierce seemed to explode. He teetered back missing much of his skull, and Jessie swiftly scrambled away as he twisted around on slackening legs, and slumped over the edge of the cliff, vanishing into the ravine's black depths. There was a soft, distant thump of meat striking rock, and then silence.

"Hang on!" Ki called. Jessie was already helping Rawhide up and along the ledge when Ki reached them. Together they made their way to where the descent looked possible. They crouched low along the slender ledge while slugs kicked up stone shards and dirt in front of their noses. The Anvil crew was firing their way, not recognizing them in the darkness; and the Block-P gunnies were pot-shooting at him too, from panic and fear of a flank attack.

Luckily the Anvil was not yet close enough, and the Block-P was too rattled to aim effectively. The twin explosions had caught both sides off balance, but the Anvil had taken immediate advantage of them, whereas the Block-P had been slow to respond. Bullets whipped through the Block-P's wounded midst, flesh and blood raining in a wide swath, and they never did fully collect their reeling wits. They began to pull back, disorganized and demoralized and leaderless, some diving for what little cover could be found, others staggering for their horses, dropping weapons, and clutching their wounds.

The descent grew easier as they neared the bowl-shaped floor. The Anvil crew was now climbing past them, keeping pressure on the Block-P, overrunning the last pockets of resistance. The Block-P fragmented, awestruck, some deserting never to return. The rest splintered into hopeless confusion.

Despite the victory of his meager Anvil band, Rawhide nonetheless breathed a vast sigh of relief when finally his boots touched solid ground at the base of the wall.

• • •

The gray light of a new dawn was just beginning to crease the eastern horizon when the Anvil bunch started back toward the ranch. The cheer at having rescued Rawhide was tempered by the high cost in life and limb, but the Block-P was broken, and Felix Pierce was gone, and that counted for a great deal.

"Speakin' of great deals," Deputy Voight said, moseying alongside Jessie and Ki, "All I got to do now is make out a report, and you'll collect a mighty big reward for recovering the gold and bringing the culprits to justice."

Ki shook his head. "Tell you what. Divvy one of those rewards between Latigo, Hicks, and Grampus. Then donate the other to Miss Wyndam."

"That ain't fair, Ki!" Voight protested. "By rights, it belongs to you."

"But Miss Wyndam has more need," Jessie responded. "I've a notion she and a certain foreman can use it to set up housekeeping proper."

"Gee," Voight said wondering. "You think Long Tom has a chance with a rich heiress like she's gonna be?"

"You'd be surprised," Ki replied softly. "They do things differently in Chicago. . . . "

SONS OF TEXAS

Book one in the exciting new saga of America's Lone Star state!

TOM EARLY

Texas, 1816. A golden land of opportunity for anyone who dared to stake a claim in its destiny...and its dangers...

Filled with action, adventure, drama and romance, *Sons of Texas* is the magnificent epic story of America in the making...the people, places, and passions that made our country great.

Look for each new book in the series!